MARIE-HÉLÈNE LEBEAULT

AUTHOR OF THE EVERS SERIES

A CURSE OF
GLASS
AND
SHADOWS

A CINDERELLA RETELLING

CHAPTER 1

THE WEIGHT OF ASH
AND GLASS

The air in the house always smelled of burning glass. Not fire or smoke—nothing so ordinary—but something sharp, metallic, and sweet. It clung to the velvet curtains like dust, curling under doors and settling into every corner. It was the scent of magic: a reminder that power hummed through every inch of the house.

Every inch except where Elysia stood.

She gripped the broom handle tightly, her hands raw and aching from a morning of scrubbing soot from the workshop floors. Lady Seraphine had given her no rest. Neither had her stepsisters. Now, in the drawing room, she was nothing more than a shadow: silent, small, unseen.

The sun poured through the tall windows, catching the delicate glass butterflies that floated lazily in the air. They gleamed like liquid silver, their wings refracting light into brilliant bursts of color. Alessa leaned back on the settee, one hand outstretched as she guided them with casual flicks of her fingers. The air around her shimmered with magic—an effortless display of wealth and talent.

"Higher, Vivienne," Alessa called, laughter lifting her voice. "You're falling behind again."

Vivienne, seated opposite her sister, scowled in concentration as molten glass dripped and coiled from her fingertips. A rose began to take shape above her hands—its petals forming slowly, glowing red-hot at the edges. She blew gently on it, and the glass cooled into something perfect: a bloom so delicate it might shatter under a breath.

"Falling behind?" Vivienne scoffed, turning the rose to catch the light. "You call that impressive? My rose will outlast your silly butterflies."

Alessa flicked her wrist, sending a butterfly to hover above Vivienne's work. Its wings stirred the air, casting tiny rainbows across the glass rose. "Beauty is fleeting, Vivienne. That's what makes it beautiful."

"Magic isn't meant to be fleeting," Vivienne shot back. "It's meant to be flawless."

Alessa flicked her fingers, sending another butterfly spiraling upward. "Fleeting or not, at least I create things that catch the eye. Tell me, Vivienne, when was the last time someone at court admired your 'precision'?"

Vivienne stiffened, her molten rose faltering for a moment before she steadied it. "Perfection speaks for itself, Alessa. Not everyone needs to dance in the spotlight to be remembered."

Elysia bit the inside of her cheek to keep from rolling her eyes. This was always the way of things—Alessa's whimsy against Vivienne's precision. They competed at everything, testing their magic like weapons disguised as art.

Magic was beauty, Elysia thought bitterly. Magic was worth. And she had none.

"Elysia!" Alessa's voice snapped across the room like a whip. "You're staring. Honestly, it's embarrassing."

Vivienne gave a little snort, turning the glass rose between her fingers. "Maybe she thinks she can learn something by watching us."

"Poor thing." Alessa's tone was all mock pity. "As if anyone without magic could ever create something." She turned her gaze back to her butterflies, letting one settle in her palm before crushing it into sparkling shards. They vanished in a puff of light, leaving nothing but the faintest hum in the air. "You can't make something from nothing, after all."

Elysia looked away, her cheeks hot. The broom felt heavier in her hands, the wood rough against her palms. She turned back to the floor and swept fiercely, forcing the ash and dust into neat little lines.

"Are you going to let her track soot across the carpet, Mother?" Vivienne asked lazily, inspecting her fingernails. The glass rose hovered nearby, catching the sunlight like a captured flame.

Lady Seraphine entered the room then, her heels clicking sharply against the marble floor. Elysia froze, the rhythm of her sweeping breaking. Lady Seraphine's gown was the color of deep wine, the glass combs in her dark hair glinting faintly with their own inner light. She was a tall woman, all sharp lines and unyielding elegance, her eyes cold and assessing.

"Vivienne," Lady Seraphine said, her voice brisk but quiet, "that rose is acceptable, but its symmetry is flawed.

The court will not forgive sloppiness, nor will I." Her gaze lingered on Vivienne's face, sharp and assessing. "You are too old for mistakes like these. Do better."

Vivienne flushed and sent the rose tumbling to the ground. It shattered into a thousand pieces, leaving glittering dust in its place. "Yes, Mother."

"Alessa," Lady Seraphine continued, "enough with your butterflies. Magic without purpose is magic wasted."

Alessa wilted slightly, her expression falling into a pout. The remaining butterflies faded, their light winking out one by one.

Lady Seraphine's gaze shifted to Elysia. For a moment, it lingered there like a shadow, heavy and suffocating. She looked her up and down—at the soot-stained apron, the worn shoes, the hair that refused to stay pinned—and her lip curled faintly, as if Elysia were something unpleasant she'd found stuck to her boot.

"And you." The words were soft, but they carried no kindness. "If you've finished playing with your broom, go to the attic and bring down the spare trunks. I won't have this house looking like a pauper's den when the court gala is announced."

Elysia dipped her head quickly. "Yes, Stepmother."

"Quickly," Lady Seraphine snapped, her eyes narrowing. "And mind your filthy hands. If I see ash on the carpet, you'll scrub it clean with your tears."

A soft, cruel laugh escaped Alessa, and Vivienne smirked, pleased to have attention shifted from her shattered rose. Elysia swallowed back the sting and turned toward the hallway. As she left the room, she heard Vivienne say, "Perhaps they'll make her sweep the streets for the prince's parade. That would suit her."

Alessa giggled, and Lady Seraphine's scolding tone faded as Elysia climbed the stairs.

———

The second floor was quieter, the house's hum of magic distant now. Sunlight strained through the stained-glass windows along the hallway, casting red and gold patches on the walls and floor. Elysia paused a moment at the window, staring at her open palms.

Empty hands.

Once, when she was small, she'd imagined there was magic buried deep in her fingers. If she squeezed them tightly enough, maybe it would spark—just a flicker, just enough to prove she belonged. But the years had stripped that hope away. Magicless. Cursed. That was what she was.

With a breath, she turned and continued up the narrow, creaking stairs toward the attic.

Filthy hands, empty hands.

Her mother had once held them and whispered, "Not all magic can be seen."

But, her mother was gone, and words were worth even less than ash.

———

The attic door groaned as Elysia pushed it open, a sound like a dying breath. Cold air spilled out to meet her, thick with the scents of mildew and forgotten things. Dust swirled in lazy patterns, disturbed only by the thin light filtering through the single round window set high in the far wall.

She hesitated at the threshold. There was something about the attic—there had always been something about the attic—that prickled at her skin. The silence was too heavy, the shadows too deep. Like the house itself held its breath here.

Elysia swallowed hard and stepped inside. The floorboards groaned beneath her feet, each step sending small puffs of dust into the air. Around her, the room sprawled like a graveyard of discarded lives: cracked trunks piled like forgotten tombstones, broken chairs with their limbs jutting at odd angles, faded draperies hanging like shrouds. She brushed past a tall, leaning cabinet, wincing as her skirts snagged on a splintered edge.

Why keep all this? she wondered. Why let it rot?

A thin shaft of sunlight spilled through the window, illuminating a trail of dust motes and broken glass. She followed it absently, her thoughts drifting to her mother, to the stories she used to tell when Elysia was small. Tales of magic hidden in plain sight, of mirrors that whispered secrets, of curses that could be broken with a single act of bravery.

Those had been nothing more than dreams, of course —soft words meant to soothe a frightened child. But, dreams had teeth when you woke up alone.

She spotted the trunks her stepmother wanted at the far side of the room, half-buried under an old sheet that hung like dead skin. Focus, she told herself. She hurried forward, reaching for the edge of the sheet to tug it free.

But something caught her eye—a flash of silver, faint and fleeting, from beneath a crumpled cloth nearby.

Elysia froze.

It wasn't much. Just a glint in the shadows, a whisper of reflected light. The sight of it sent a shiver up her spine, and her fingers went cold. She turned her head slowly, drawn toward the source, until she was staring at a shape half-hidden beneath the sheet.

It was tall and wide, propped against the wall like a sentry left to keep watch. The fabric draped over it stirred faintly, though there was no breeze. For a long moment, Elysia simply stood there, her breath shallow, her hands clenched at her sides.

"Don't be ridiculous," she whispered to herself. But, the words felt thin, weak, even as she forced her feet to move.

Step by step, she approached the shape. Her heart drummed against her ribs, loud in the silence. She reached out and caught the edge of the cloth, her fingers trembling. She tugged the sheet with deliberate slowness, the fabric resisting as though it clung to the secrets beneath. Dust and cobwebs fell like ash, clouding the air. She stifled a cough, her focus locked on what lay beneath. The mirror glimmered faintly, its frame catching the dim light like silver spun from shadows. Elysia stepped back, her pulse roaring in her ears. This was no ordinary relic.

The sheet fell away, a cascade of dust and cobwebs, and the mirror was revealed.

Elysia's breath hitched, her heart hammering in her chest. She hesitated, fingers trembling on the edge of the sheet. She glanced over her shoulder, the silent attic pressing against her. A faint creak from below sent a jolt of panic through her limbs. What if they heard her? What if her stepmother caught her here, caught her touching things that didn't belong to her? She clenched her fists, forcing the fear aside. They wouldn't come. They never came up here.

It was beautiful—horribly, impossibly beautiful.

The frame was silver, chased with patterns of curling vines and sharp-edged thorns. They twisted and spiraled toward the center, where they melted into the smooth, perfect glass. But, the surface was unlike any mirror Elysia had ever seen. It wasn't silvered and clear; it was dark, like still water at midnight, or polished obsidian. It did not reflect the room around it. It reflected nothing at all.

Elysia's mouth went dry. What is this?

She knelt slowly, her skirts pooling around her. She raised a shaking hand to touch the glass, half-expecting it to burn her fingers. Elysia hesitated, her fingers hovering over the dark, liquid-like surface. A memory flickered in her mind: her mother's hands, clasping her own. "Not all magic can be seen. Some of it is quiet. Some of it is hidden. But, it's always there, waiting," her mother had whispered once, years ago, as they knelt together by a garden bed of frost-kissed glass flowers. Her mother's warmth was a distant echo now, as fleeting as a dream.

The surface was cool, impossibly smooth. Her reflection began to take shape—dim, hazy, as though seen through a thick fog. She frowned, leaning closer. It wasn't the face she expected. The girl staring back at her was pale, small, and trembling—a shadow, barely formed. Elysia's throat tightened. Was this how the world saw her? Was this how she saw herself?

The reflection rippled, the haze twisting into new shapes. A faint smile formed—a mockery of her own expression. "Is that who you are?" the girl in the glass seemed to whisper, though no sound left its lips.

The reflection sharpened. And smiled.

Elysia gasped, stumbling back, her hand flying to her mouth. The girl in the glass—her reflection—didn't move as she did. It stared back at her with pale, unblinking eyes and a faint, knowing smile.

"What…" Her voice cracked, and the word died in the shadows.

The reflection rippled, as though the glass had turned to liquid. The face twisted, reshaping itself like smoke blown apart. The girl's features melted away, replaced by something else—someone else.

A man.

He was sharp where she was soft, the planes of his face defined, his dark hair falling in untidy waves across his forehead. His eyes were black as the glass itself, though they caught faint sparks of silver when he blinked. He tilted his head, his mouth curving into a smirk that sent ice down Elysia's spine.

"Well," he said, his voice soft and curling like smoke, "it's about time."

Elysia couldn't breathe. She couldn't move.

"Who…" She swallowed, her voice barely more than a whisper. "Who are you?"

The man in the mirror raised an eyebrow. "Is that really the first question you want to ask me?"

Elysia stared at him, her heart pounding in her chest like a caged bird. "You're... you're in the mirror."

"Very observant," he drawled, his smile widening to reveal teeth a shade too sharp. "And here I thought you were just another girl sent up to dust off the relics."

Elysia bristled despite herself. "I'm not—" She stopped, unsure what she meant to say.

The man—the voice in the mirror—sighed, his expression turning almost bored. "Let's skip the introductions, shall we? I know who you are, little cinder-girl."

That word again. Cinder-girl. It sent a flare of anger through her chest.

"And you?" she asked, forcing her voice to steady. "Who are you?"

The man leaned forward, though the glass between them did not shift. For a moment, Elysia thought he might reach through it, though no hand emerged. "I've been called many things," he said, his tone almost playful. "A mage. A prisoner. A liar. A curse."

Elysia blinked, her stomach twisting. "A curse?"

"Of sorts." He tilted his head, his dark eyes glinting. "But, you can call me Caius."

The name settled into the air like dust.

Caius smiled again, slower this time, and Elysia's skin prickled. "Tell me, little cinder-girl," he asked softly, "do you want to break your curse?"

"Yes," she whispered, though her throat tightened at the thought.

"Good." His reflection sharpened, his dark eyes gleaming. "But, be careful what you wish for, little cinder-girl.

The court is not what you think it is. Their magic may glitter, but beneath it lies rot."

"What do you mean?"

He smirked faintly, though there was no humor in it. "You'll see," he said simply, the mirror rippling faintly.

Elysia stared at him, her heart racing. She didn't answer right away. The words hung in the air, heavy with promise, but beneath them, she heard something else—a whisper of risk, of consequence. She thought of her mother's voice: "Not all magic can be seen." Was this what her mother had meant? This strange, beautiful darkness shimmering in the mirror? Or was she reaching for something that might shatter her instead? Her lips parted, but no words came.

Do you want to break your curse? the man had asked.

The embers inside her stirred, fragile and flickering, and somewhere deep in her chest, the thought found root —yes.

———

The attic grew colder, though Elysia couldn't tell if it was the room or the weight of Caius's words pressing down on her.

Do you want to break your curse?

The question lingered like smoke in her mind, curling around every corner of her thoughts and snuffing out reason. She stared at the mirror—the dark glass that swallowed the light—and at the man within it. His gaze, black and sharp as obsidian, held hers with an intensity that felt like a blade poised at her throat.

Finally, she found her voice. "What do you know about my curse?"

Caius smiled again, but it was not a kind smile. It was the sort of smile you might offer someone standing at the edge of a cliff. "I know it binds you," he said softly, "as surely as this glass binds me."

Elysia swallowed, her throat dry. "What do you mean?"

"Your family," Caius continued, leaning back into the shadows, though his eyes never left her. "Magicless, empty. Not by chance, little cinder-girl. By design."

Caius's smirk flickered, his voice dropping lower. "Curses are curious things, don't you think? Some bind bloodlines, others, individuals. And sometimes..." His dark gaze sharpened. "Sometimes they're two sides of the same coin." He leaned closer, the glass shimmering. "I was once a master of glass, Elysia. My power shaped empires, until it was used to cage me. Tell me, little cinder-girl—if you break your chains, who else might you free?"

Elysia's pulse quickened. "You're lying."

"Am I?" Caius tilted his head, his dark hair spilling forward like shadows. "You live in a kingdom where power flows like water through the hands of even the lowest beggar. Do you think it's an accident that yours were born dry?"

Elysia flinched. "Why would anyone curse us?"

"Why does anyone do anything?" Caius replied. "Greed, pride, vengeance. I could name a dozen reasons, but I doubt the truth would soothe you." He smiled faintly. "What matters is that the curse exists. And curses, Elysia..." he paused, his voice dropping to a near whisper, "curses can be broken."

The embers inside her flickered. Hope—small, danger-ous, and utterly foolish—stirred in her chest. She clenched her hands into fists, her nails biting into her skin.

"What are you?" she asked. "How do you know so much about my family?"

Caius's smile faded. For a moment, something unread-able flashed across his face—a shadow of regret, perhaps, or something darker. "I am a mage," he said at last, his voice low. "Or I was. Once."

Elysia glanced down at the glass surface. It was so still, so perfect, it seemed to swallow the very idea of motion. "You're trapped."

"Very observant," Caius said dryly. "It seems even the cinder-girl has her moments."

"Why?" she pressed, ignoring the barb. "Who put you here?"

Caius's expression darkened, the gleam in his eyes turning to something sharp and dangerous. "Those who feared me," he said. "Those who wished to take what I had and bury me for eternity in a cage of glass and shadow."

Elysia stared at him, her heart pounding. She wanted to look away, to break free from his gaze, but something about him held her fast. "You want me to free you."

Caius's smile returned, slow and sharp. "It seems we understand each other."

Elysia took a step back. "No. I—I can't. I don't even know you."

"Don't you?" Caius's voice softened, his words curling like smoke in the air. "You know what it is to be small, don't you? To live in the shadow of others, to be nothing more than dust on their boots? I can see it in your eyes, Elysia. You want to be more. You deserve to be more."

The truth of it hit her like a blow. It was what she'd never dared to say aloud, not even in the quiet of her own mind. She hated the way her stepmother looked at her, as if she were a stain on the floor that couldn't be scrubbed clean. She hated the way Alessa and Vivienne flaunted their power, twisting glass into wonders while she swept up the broken pieces. She hated the emptiness she felt, the hollow ache that came from being nothing and no one.

And more than anything, she hated that it was true.

She did want to be more.

Caius seemed to sense the shift in her, because his smile widened, and his voice dropped to a whisper. "I can help you, Elysia. I can teach you what they would never dare to teach. Power flows through glass like blood through veins. I can show you how to shape it, bend it, make it your own."

Elysia's breath caught. "Glass magic?"

"Yes," Caius said, his dark eyes glinting. "The very thing they use to keep you small. The very thing they hoard and guard so jealously. It could be yours. You could shatter the chains they've wrapped around you."

She looked down at her hands—small, calloused, empty. She had spent her whole life watching others wield glass as though it were an extension of themselves, while she could only clean the remnants of their failures. The thought of holding magic in her own hands, of bending glass to her will, was almost too much to imagine.

But, she knew better than to trust a man who smiled from behind a mirror.

"What do you get in return?" she asked.

Caius's smile didn't waver. "What do I want?" He spread his hands, a gesture of mock innocence. "Freedom, of course. Break the mirror, and I am free. That is all I ask."

"What happens when you're free?"

Caius tilted his head, his smile turning faintly wolfish. "That is not your concern."

Elysia's heart pounded in her chest. Every instinct she had told her to turn and run, to leave the mirror where it was and never look back. But, she couldn't. Not when he was offering her the one thing she'd always wanted: a chance to break free.

"I'll think about it," she said at last.

Caius's smile widened, his teeth catching the faint light like shards of glass. "Take your time, little cinder-girl. I'm not going anywhere."

The glass wavered again, as though stirred by an unseen hand, and then his reflection dissolved, leaving Elysia staring at her own pale face.

Her heart still racing, she turned away, the weight of what had just happened pressing down on her shoulders. She grabbed the trunks her stepmother had asked for, her mind a storm of questions she couldn't answer.

As she left the attic, she cast one last glance at the mirror. It sat there in the corner, silent and still, its surface still smooth and dark as a pool of ink.

But, she swore she could still feel Caius's eyes on her back, watching.

Waiting.

CHAPTER 2

WHISPERS OF GLASS

The house was silent, save for the groan of old wood and the occasional rattle of glass in its frames. The darkness outside pressed close against the windows, as though the night itself watched and waited. Elysia moved carefully through the halls, her footsteps light and soundless on the worn floors.

It was nearly midnight.

She paused at the base of the attic stairs, her heart thrumming in her chest. In the stillness, it was so loud she feared it might give her away. She cast a glance over her shoulder, straining her ears for any sound—Alessa's laughter, Vivienne's biting remarks, Lady Seraphine's cold voice.

But, the house slept.

Drawing a shallow breath, Elysia turned back to the stairs. Her hand trembled on the banister as she climbed, the wood creaking beneath her weight. Elysia ascended into another world, each step carrying her farther from the familiar warmth of the kitchen hearth and deeper into shadows that seemed to swallow the light.

By the time she reached the attic door, her hands were clammy and cold. She hesitated, staring at the tarnished brass handle. What am I doing?

The question gnawed at her like a rat. This was madness—whispered voices in a mirror, promises made by a man she didn't know. She should have left the mirror covered in its sheet, forgotten and buried like everything else in this house. She should have run.

But she hadn't.

Elysia glanced down at her hands, remembering the laughter of her stepsisters, the glass butterflies that danced like jewels in the air, and her stepmother's scornful gaze. She clenched her fingers into fists. Her hands felt like shadows—empty of power, empty of purpose.

But as her thoughts darkened, the air seemed to shift. A vibration trembled beneath her skin, faint and insistent, like the pluck of an unseen string. The shards scattered across the hallway shivered as though caught in a breath of wind. She scrambled to still her thoughts, forcing herself to focus, to calm. The hum faded—but not before she heard Vivienne's voice echo faintly from the drawing room. "Did you hear that?"

With a shuddering breath, she pushed the door open.

The attic's chill pressed against her skin, biting through the thin fabric of her dress. Dust hung in the air, unmoving, like the room had been frozen in time. The mirror sat exactly where she had left it, its silver frame glinting faintly in the moonlight filtering through the small, round window.

The glass seemed to breathe as she entered, its surface fluttering faintly, like water disturbed by a whisper.

"Back so soon?" Caius's voice curled through the room like smoke. The surface of the mirror shifted, and his face emerged from the darkness within—sharp and pale, his black eyes gleaming faintly, as though they held their own light.

Elysia froze in the doorway, the handle still gripped in her hand. "I shouldn't be here."

"No, you shouldn't," Caius replied, tilting his head. His voice was smooth, soft, and unnervingly amused. "Yet, here you are. Curious, isn't it?"

Elysia swallowed hard, forcing her feet to carry her closer. The mirror loomed larger with every step, its surface so dark it seemed to devour the light. When she was close enough, she could see her reflection again—dim and shadowed, her face pale with fear. And beyond it, Caius watched her, his expression unreadable.

"What do you want from me?" she asked, her voice barely above a whisper.

Caius leaned forward, his face filling the glass. "I already told you. I want freedom. You want magic. We can help each other, little cinder-girl. Or have you forgotten already?"

Elysia bristled at the name, but she said nothing.

"Why me?" she pressed. "Why now?"

"Why not?" Caius countered, a faint smile tugging at his lips. "Do you think you're the first to find me? You aren't. But, you are the first to come back."

His words sent a chill up her spine. "What happened to the others?"

Caius's smile widened, though it held no warmth. "They weren't ready."

"Ready for what?"

"To take what they want." His voice dropped, low and coaxing. "Power is not for the timid, Elysia. It is not given; it is taken. And you..." He tilted his head, studying her. "You want to take it, don't you?"

She looked away, her cheeks burning. "I just want to break the curse."

"You think that makes you different?" Caius's voice turned sharper, his amusement fraying at the edges. "Everyone wants something, girl. Freedom, vengeance, love—it doesn't matter. The question isn't what you want. It's what you're willing to give."

Elysia's gaze snapped back to his, anger sparking in her chest. "I have nothing to give."

Caius's expression stilled, his dark eyes pinning her in place. "Then, you have nothing to lose."

The words hit her like a blow. She opened her mouth to argue, but no words came. Because deep down, she knew he was right. She had nothing—no magic, no status, no family worth the name. She was a servant in her own home, forgotten and despised. What could she possibly lose that hadn't already been taken?

Caius's voice softened. "I can teach you, Elysia. I can give you the power to break your chains. To shatter the curse that keeps you small." He paused, and his voice dropped to a whisper. "But, you must choose. I cannot make you."

Elysia looked down at her hands, pale and trembling. For as long as she could remember, she had dreamed of this—of having something that was hers, something that no one could take away. Magic. Power. A way to be more than a shadow in her stepmother's house.

But, the mirror's surface ebbed and flowed faintly, and she couldn't shake the feeling that she stood on the edge of a precipice. One step closer, and she would fall.

"What do I have to do?" she asked.

Caius smiled, slow and satisfied. "Touch the glass."

Elysia hesitated, her breath caught in her throat. The surface of the mirror seemed to shift, as though the shadows within it moved and breathed. She raised her hand slowly, her fingers trembling, until they hovered just above the glass. It was so close she could feel the cold radiating from it, like the air before a storm.

"One touch," Caius said softly. "One step. And there's no turning back."

Elysia's heart thundered in her chest. She thought of Alessa's butterflies, Vivienne's roses, Lady Seraphine's cold voice and colder eyes. She thought of the empty years stretching out before her, filled with nothing but ash and silence.

I won't live like this, she thought fiercely. Not anymore.

Before she could change her mind, she pressed her palm against the glass.

The surface was freezing. It rippled like water under her touch, and for one terrible moment, she felt as though she were sinking into it—into the darkness, the cold, the stillness. A faint thread of light flared beneath her hand, spreading outward like cracks in ice.

Caius's voice echoed faintly, as though coming from far away. "Well done, little cinder-girl. Well done."

Elysia pulled her hand back with a gasp, stumbling

away from the mirror. The light faded, and the glass stilled, leaving nothing but her reflection staring back at her—pale, wide-eyed, and trembling.

"What... what was that?" she whispered.

Caius smiled, his black eyes gleaming. "The first step. The bond is made."

Elysia stared at him, her chest rising and falling in shallow breaths. The cold still lingered in her fingers, as though the mirror had left its mark. "What now?"

"Now," Caius said softly, "we begin."

———

The garden shed was cold and silent, its wooden walls groaning faintly in the night wind. Elysia sat on the dirt floor, the smell of damp earth thick in the air, her hands trembling in her lap. She had chosen this place carefully—far enough from the house that no one would hear her, small enough to feel hidden. The broken tools and forgotten pots were her only company, save for the faint, mocking hum of Caius's voice.

"Are you ready, little cinder-girl?"

His voice echoed from the mirror she'd dragged here in secret. It sat propped against the wall, dark and still, a pool of shadow in the moonlit shed. Caius's face hovered just beneath the surface, his expression unreadable.

Elysia swallowed, curling her fingers against her palms. Her hands still ached from earlier, the ghost of the mirror's cold lingering in her skin. She thought of Alessa and Vivienne, their magic dancing like light on water, and of her stepmother's voice: You will always be empty.

"I'm ready," she said, though her voice shook.

Caius's eyes narrowed, gleaming faintly in the darkness. "We'll see."

He leaned closer, his pale face filling the glass. "Glass magic is not like other magics. It is sharp, alive. It bends only to those who are stronger than it. If you hesitate, it will cut you. If you falter, it will shatter."

"I understand," Elysia said, though the cold knot of fear in her stomach told her otherwise.

"Do you?" Caius murmured, tilting his head. "We'll start small. Find a shard."

Elysia glanced around the shed. By the moonlight filtering through a crack in the roof, she spotted the remnants of a glass jar lying broken in the corner. She crawled over and picked up one of the pieces, careful not to slice her fingers. It was small and jagged, no longer smooth, but it caught the light in a way that made it look almost alive.

She held it up to the mirror. "Will this work?"

Caius studied it, his dark eyes gleaming. "It will do. Sit down and listen carefully."

Elysia obeyed, crossing her legs on the floor, the shard resting in her open palm. It felt heavier than it should, its edges biting into her skin.

"Close your eyes," Caius commanded. "And breathe."

Elysia hesitated, then obeyed. The darkness behind her eyelids was thick and suffocating, and the cold seeped deeper into her bones.

"Glass hums," Caius said softly, his voice weaving through the silence. "It sings to those who know how to listen. Can you hear it?"

23

Elysia frowned, her brow furrowing. "I don't—"

"Quiet." Caius's voice was sharp, a whipcrack in the stillness. "Listen."

She swallowed her protest and focused. At first, there was nothing. Just the faint creak of the shed and the thud of her own heartbeat. She tightened her grip on the shard, willing herself to hear something.

And then...

A faint sound, almost too soft to notice. A hum, low and melodic, like a string vibrating in an empty room. It thrummed in her palm, a pulse she could feel more than hear, and Elysia gasped, her eyes snapping open.

"I heard it," she whispered.

Caius smiled, sharp and cold. "Good. Now command it."

"Command it?"

"Glass obeys will," he said. "Shape it. Bend it. Make it more than it is."

"Is that what the court does?" Elysia asked cautiously. "Shape magic, bend it to their will?"

Caius's gaze darkened. "The court consumes magic. They take what they want and leave nothing but ash. They would do the same to you if they discovered your curse."

Elysia frowned. "But, curses can be broken, can't they? Isn't that why I need the prince?"

"Curses," Caius said, his voice curling with disdain, "are not simple things to untangle. They linger like shadows, even when the light is gone. Most people fear them, avoid them. But you..." he paused, his tone sharpening, "you think they'll see you as something more than a liability?"

Her throat tightened at his words, but she refused to look away.

Elysia stared at the shard, her pulse quickening. "How?"

"Picture what you want," Caius said. "Hold it in your mind like a flame. The glass will listen. It will follow."

She took a shaky breath, closing her eyes again. Her fingers curled around the shard, and she focused on the hum, on the way it seemed to vibrate in time with her heartbeat. Picture it, she thought. Something small. Something beautiful.

A butterfly.

She remembered Alessa's butterflies—delicate, glowing, perfect. Elysia gripped the shard tighter, ignoring the sting as it bit into her skin. In her mind, she saw it clearly: wings fine as silk, the light of the moon caught in its veins.

The shard in her hand began to tremble.

"Yes," Caius murmured, his voice low with satisfaction. "There it is. Don't stop now."

Elysia gripped the shard tighter. She thought of the butterfly—its delicate wings, its shimmering light. But as she focused, her frustration bled into the image. The butterfly became jagged, its edges too sharp, its light flickering like a dying flame. The hum in her palm swelled, louder and harsher, until it drowned out everything else.

"Stop!" Caius's voice snapped, sharp and commanding. Elysia's eyes flew open just as the shard in her hand exploded. The fragments slashed across her palm, scattering onto the floor in a burst of harsh light.

"Foolish girl," Caius growled. "Do you think glass will

obey chaos? It mirrors your heart. If you cannot control yourself, you cannot control it."

Elysia's chest heaved as she cradled her bleeding hand. Her gaze dropped to the scattered shards, but they didn't lie still—they trembled faintly, the hum still pulsing in the air. She bit back a sob and forced herself to look away.

For a moment, the broken shards caught the faint candlelight, scattering reflections across the walls and ceiling. Her gaze darted to one fragment lying closest to her, where her face stared back in warped, jagged pieces. She hated what she saw—a girl who had failed again, who couldn't even hold a single spark of magic without breaking it.

But as she reached for the jagged shard, her mother's voice whispered, soft but unrelenting, "Not all magic can be seen." Her reflection glimmered faintly in the glass shard, no longer a single, broken face but a kaleidoscope of shifting shapes and light. Perhaps... perhaps there was more to her than what the glass showed. Perhaps there was more to her than she dared to see.

"You broke it," Caius said flatly, his words sharp as glass.

"I—" Her breath trembled as she stared at the fragment in her hand, its edge biting into her skin. "I tried. I felt the hum. I thought—" Her voice broke, and her fingers curled around the shard she'd picked up. The piece seemed to mock her, gleaming faintly in the moonlight. "You'll always be nothing." Alessa's laughter echoed in her memory. For a moment, she believed it. But then, her anger flared, quiet but steady, like the glow of embers in ash. "I'll do better."

"Trying isn't enough," Caius said. "Do you think magic bends to the will of the weak? It doesn't. If you want it, you must take it."

Elysia's breath hitched, her hands trembling as she grasped the shard tighter. "What if I'm not strong enough?" she whispered. The words spilled out before she could stop them, raw and aching.

Caius tilted his head, his dark eyes gleaming. "Glass doesn't care about your strength. It reflects what's inside you—fear, anger, hope. It doesn't lie."

He stepped closer, the mirror billowing softly with his movements. "Do you know what I see when I look at you?"

Elysia flinched but forced herself to meet his gaze. "What?" she asked, her voice barely steady.

"A girl who is so desperate to be something more that she's forgotten who she is," Caius said. "You think power will make them see you. You think it will give you worth. All it does is reveal what's already there. So, tell me—what do you see when you look at yourself?"

Her throat tightened as her mind conjured the answer unbidden: a girl draped in ash and failure, hollow-eyed and trembling. "I don't know," she whispered.

"Then learn," Caius snapped. "Pain is a teacher, Elysia. Use it."

She looked down at the glass shards, her vision swimming. The ache in her hand was sharp and insistent, but beneath it, something else stirred. The memory of the hum, the way it had answered her call. The way it had almost obeyed.

She reached for another shard.

Caius's smile returned, faint and wolfish. "Good. Again."

Elysia held the shard tightly, ignoring the blood smeared on its edges. She closed her eyes, the butterfly clear in her mind's eye, and reached for the hum.

The sun had just begun to rise, its pale light crawling across the horizon, when Elysia slipped back into the house. She moved carefully, one hand pressed against the wall to steady herself. Her body ached with exhaustion, her head pounding from a night spent trying—and failing—to master Caius's magic.

Her hands throbbed the most. The cuts from the shattered glass stung like fire, each one a reminder of how far she still had to go. She kept her fingers curled to hide the worst of the damage, though the blood was already soaking through the edges of her sleeves.

The house was still quiet. The servants wouldn't be stirring for another hour, and her stepmother and stepsisters were surely still asleep. Elysia crept into the kitchen, the familiar smell of ashes and burnt wood grounding her as she crossed to the basin in the corner. She turned the pump handle carefully, wincing as water splashed into the stone bowl.

Her breath hissed through her teeth as she plunged her hands beneath the stream. The cold bit into her skin, setting the cuts ablaze, but she didn't pull back. She scrubbed quickly, washing away the blood and bits of glass, ignoring the dark water swirling down the drain.

You broke it, Caius's voice echoed in her mind, sharp as the glass that had shattered in her palm. If you want magic, Elysia, you must take it.

She could still hear the hum of the glass, faint and mocking, as if it had slipped just beyond her reach. She had tried so hard—her mind fixed on the image of the butterfly, on the way it might have glimmered in her palm. For one moment, it had felt possible. For one moment, the magic had been hers.

But then, it had broken. And so had she.

Elysia pressed her hands to the cloth towel by the basin, watching the fabric turn red. Her reflection stared back at her faintly from the windowpane above the sink— pale and hollow-eyed, with strands of hair escaping her braid.

She had looked like this for years: tired, forgotten, small. But, something had shifted in the dark of the shed, in the hum of the glass. She couldn't unhear it. She couldn't ignore the truth that had settled in her chest like a burning coal.

She would go back. She had to go back.

The kitchen door creaked open behind her. Elysia froze, her heart leaping into her throat as she turned quickly, shoving her hands behind her back.

Alessa stood in the doorway, draped in a pale silk dressing gown. Her dark hair tumbled over her shoulders in loose waves, and she looked as pristine as if she'd been painted there. She blinked sleepily at Elysia, then arched a delicate eyebrow.

"What are you doing?"

"Nothing." The lie was out before Elysia could stop it. "I—I was just cleaning."

Alessa's gaze drifted to the basin, then to Elysia's rumpled dress and the towel streaked with red. Her eyes narrowed. "What's that on your sleeve?"

Elysia swallowed, stepping back toward the basin to block her view. "It's nothing. Just a—just a scratch."

"A scratch?" Alessa's lips curled faintly. "From what? Did you try to fight off a broom?"

Elysia didn't answer. Her pulse thundered in her ears, and she fought the urge to glance at the clock. If Alessa caught her sneaking around the house in the dead of night, or worse, found the mirror in the shed, it would all be over.

"Why are you always so strange?" Alessa continued, wrinkling her nose as she padded toward the table. "You disappear for hours, sneaking around like a rat, and you look even filthier than usual." She dropped into a chair, draping herself across the table with theatrical boredom. "Honestly, it's pathetic."

Elysia bit the inside of her cheek to keep from snapping back. She couldn't risk it. Not now. She grabbed the towel and turned her back on Alessa, wringing it tightly in her hands.

"Mother won't be happy if she catches you slinking around again," Alessa went on. "I might tell her, you know."

"I haven't done anything wrong," Elysia said quietly.

Alessa laughed, the sound sharp as breaking glass. "You exist, don't you? That's wrong enough."

The words stung, but Elysia didn't let it show. She

30

turned back to the basin, rinsing her hands again just to have something to do. The water was clear now, though her skin still burned, the cuts raw and angry.

"Alessa?"

The new voice made Elysia's stomach twist. Vivienne swept into the kitchen, her hair pinned back neatly, though she was still in her nightclothes. She glanced between Alessa and Elysia, her sharp gaze lingering on the towel Elysia clutched.

"What's going on?"

"Nothing," Alessa said breezily, resting her chin in her hand. "Elysia was just skulking around again."

Vivienne frowned. "Why are you bleeding?"

Elysia froze. Vivienne's eyes had caught the edge of her sleeve, where a faint smear of red still clung to the fabric. Before Elysia could pull her arm back, Vivienne reached out and grabbed her wrist, yanking her hand into view.

Elysia gasped, biting back a cry as pain flared through her palm.

Vivienne's lips parted, her frown deepening as she turned Elysia's hand over. The cuts crisscrossed her skin like tiny scars, dark and ugly against her pale flesh. Vivienne glanced up sharply, her eyes narrowing. "What did you do?"

"It's nothing," Elysia said quickly, tugging her arm back. "I cut myself cleaning the shed."

"The shed?" Vivienne's gaze turned suspicious. "Why were you in the shed in the middle of the night?"

Elysia's mind raced. "I—I was looking for tools. Stepmother wanted me to—"

"Enough."

The voice cut through the room like a blade. Lady Seraphine stood in the doorway, her gown a rich, heavy green that seemed to drink the light. Her sharp gaze swept across the scene before settling on Elysia, who quickly lowered her head.

"What is this noise?" Lady Seraphine demanded.

"Elysia was sneaking around again," Vivienne said, her voice smooth and clipped. "She's hurt herself doing something ridiculous."

Lady Seraphine's eyes narrowed. "Show me."

Elysia hesitated, but she knew better than to disobey. She stepped forward and extended her hand, palm up, for her stepmother to see. Lady Seraphine studied the cuts, her expression betraying nothing.

"Clumsy," she said at last, her voice cold. "And careless." She let Elysia's hand drop. "Clean yourself up and see that you don't bleed on the floors. I won't have this house looking like a slaughterhouse."

"Yes, Stepmother," Elysia murmured, her voice tight.

Lady Seraphine turned away, her skirts sweeping across the stone floor. "Vivienne, Alessa—go and dress for the day. I won't have you lazing about like children."

The stepsisters cast Elysia one last glance—Alessa's mocking, Vivienne's suspicious—before following their mother out of the kitchen.

Elysia stood alone, her hand still throbbing, the silence pressing down on her. She turned back to the basin, splashing water onto her face, her breath shaky and uneven.

It's worth it, she told herself, clinging to the memory of the glass shard humming in her palm. It has to be worth it.

But as she wrung the bloodstained towel out for the last time, she couldn't help but wonder how much more the magic would take before it gave anything back.

CHAPTER 3
SHARDS OF POWER

The garden shed felt colder tonight, as though the walls were holding their breath. Elysia sat cross-legged on the dirt floor, the mirror propped against the wall before her. A single candle flickered nearby, its flame barely cutting through the shadows.

Caius's face hovered just beneath the surface of the glass, his dark eyes watching her intently. He looked sharper than before—his features edged like glass, his smile faint and cutting.

"You look tired," he said, his voice curling through the air like smoke. "Not losing your nerve, are you?"

"No," Elysia said quickly, though her hands shook as they rested in her lap. The cuts from the night before still throbbed, hidden beneath fresh bandages.

Caius arched an eyebrow. "Good. If you're going to waste my time, I'd rather know now."

Elysia bit the inside of her cheek. She didn't dare argue with him, not when he was her only chance—her only hope of becoming something more than ash and dust. "What do you want me to do?"

"Finally, a useful question." Caius leaned back slightly, his reflection shifting as though the glass were water. "Tonight, you will shape the glass."

She hesitated. "What if it breaks again?"

"Then it breaks." Caius's voice turned sharp, like a blade pressed against her skin. "Magic doesn't reward the timid, Elysia. You failed because you were afraid. You hesitated. Glass obeys strength and will—not uncertainty."

Elysia's fists clenched. He was right, though she hated him for saying it. She had hesitated, afraid of the hum, of the power sparking beneath her skin. Afraid of what it might mean if she succeeded.

"I'll try again," she said, lifting her chin.

Caius's smile widened. "Good. Then we begin."

Elysia reached into her pocket and pulled out the shard of glass she'd brought with her—a small piece, no larger than her thumb. It was smooth on one side, jagged on the other, and it glimmered faintly in the candlelight. She set it on the floor in front of her, feeling its weight, the cool edge of it against her skin.

"Close your eyes," Caius said softly. "You remember the hum, don't you? The way the glass sings when you listen?"

She nodded, shutting her eyes. The darkness felt heavier tonight, pressing against her like a second skin.

"Good," Caius murmured. "Now listen. Feel it."

Elysia inhaled slowly, her heartbeat loud in her ears. She focused on the shard, on the cool memory of glass against her palm, on the way it had vibrated like a living thing. At first, there was nothing—just the silence of the shed and the distant whisper of wind. But then, it came: the hum.

Soft at first, so faint she thought she might be imagining it. It grew louder as she focused, a low note that seemed to tremble in the air, weaving itself around her bones. She felt it in her hands, in her chest, like the deep vibration of a bell.

"Yes," Caius whispered. "There it is. Now, command it."

Elysia frowned. "How?"

"You know how," Caius said sharply. "Will it into shape. See it in your mind. Feel it. The glass is alive, Elysia. Bend it. Make it yours."

She gritted her teeth, clutching the shard tighter. Her mind reached for the image she had chosen before: a butterfly. She pictured it clearly—the curve of the wings, the thin, delicate veins, the way it might shimmer like water caught in moonlight.

"Focus," Caius urged. "Don't let it slip away."

The hum grew louder, sharper. Her fingers tingled as the shard grew warm, then hot, the heat spreading up her palms and into her arms. Elysia gasped, but she didn't let go. The image in her mind wavered, but she held onto it desperately, forcing the glass to listen, to change.

For one terrible moment, she thought it would shatter again. The hum swelled, shrill and deafening, the glass vibrating so violently it felt as though it might tear itself apart. Her hands burned, her body trembling with the effort, but she pushed.

And then—

Silence.

The hum stopped. The heat vanished. The air went still.

Elysia opened her eyes, her breath catching in her throat.

The shard was gone. In its place, resting in her cupped hands, was a butterfly.

It was small—no larger than her palm—and imperfect, its wings uneven and the edges rough where the glass hadn't smoothed completely. But, it was whole. It caught the candlelight as though it had been carved from liquid moonlight, gleaming softly in the dark.

"I did it," she whispered, her voice breaking. "I did it."

Caius watched her from the mirror, his expression unreadable. For a long moment, he said nothing. Then, slowly, he smiled. "Well done."

Elysia looked up at him, surprise flickering across her face. It was the first time he had praised her—truly praised her.

"You have the spark," Caius said, his voice soft but deliberate. "I can see it in you now. You are not as weak as I thought."

The words should have stung, but they didn't. Not tonight. Elysia looked back at the butterfly in her hands, her chest swelling with something she couldn't name. Pride. Power. Hope.

But, the butterfly trembled.

Elysia frowned, watching as faint cracks began to spread across the glass, like frost creeping across a windowpane.

"Wait—"

The butterfly shattered.

Glass splinters exploded in her hands, sharp and sudden. Elysia cried out, dropping the shards onto the dirt floor as blood bloomed across her palms.

"Pathetic," Caius snapped, his voice like a whip. "You lost control. I warned you—glass does not forgive weakness."

Elysia blinked back tears, cradling her bleeding hands to her chest. "But I—I made it."

"And then, you broke it." Caius's face was sharp with disdain. "Do you want to waste this chance, Elysia? Do you want to stay small forever?"

"No," she said fiercely, though her voice trembled.

"Then stop sniveling," Caius said coldly. "Clean your hands. Rest. And when you come back tomorrow, be stronger."

The mirror's surface rippled, and Caius's face disappeared, leaving Elysia staring at her own reflection—pale, hollow-eyed, and bleeding.

She sat there for a long moment, the silence pressing down on her like a weight. Finally, she picked up one of the shards from the ground, turning it over in her fingers. It was small and sharp, but it glimmered faintly in the candlelight.

She closed her hand around it, letting the edge bite into her skin.

Next time, she thought. I will not fail.

The first blush of dawn crept through the cracks in the shutters, pale light slanting across the small, stone-walled room. Elysia slipped inside as quietly as a whisper, closing the door behind her with a trembling hand.

Her body ached with every step—her muscles heavy, her limbs leaden—and her hands stung with a relentless, burning throb. She sank onto the edge of the narrow cot in the corner of the room, letting her head fall forward, her breath shuddering out in uneven bursts.

One night, she thought. Just one night.

Her sleeves were still damp with blood, the fabric sticking to her skin. Carefully, she unwrapped the bandages around her hands, wincing as the cloth pulled at the cuts across her palms. The wounds were deeper this time, angry red gashes surrounded by swelling and faint bruises. Tiny splinters of glass still clung to her skin, glittering faintly in the dim light like shards of stars.

Her throat tightened. She had made something. For one brief, perfect moment, she had held magic in her hands. A butterfly, fragile and shivering, but real. And then, it had broken.

I broke it.

Elysia clenched her fists, despite the pain, her bloodied hands shaking in her lap. She could still feel the hum of the glass, a faint vibration echoing in her memory. It had been alive, warm, singing to her as though it wanted to obey—until she had lost control.

Caius's words rang in her ears: "Magic doesn't reward the timid."

She reached into her pocket and pulled out a small shard of glass she had taken from the shed floor. It was sharp and jagged, but she turned it over in her fingers, watching the way it caught the light filtering through the shutters. It looked harmless now—just a broken thing, discarded and forgotten.

Like her.

She pressed her thumb against the sharpest edge, letting it bite into her skin until a single drop of blood bloomed against its surface.

"You are not weak," she whispered to herself, the words fierce and low. She stared at the shard, as though willing it to understand. "I will not fail again."

But, her voice cracked on the last word, and she swallowed hard, closing her eyes. The weight of the night settled over her like a lead cloak, pressing into her ribs until it hurt to breathe.

The quiet was shattered by the faint creak of a floorboard outside the door.

Elysia's head snapped up, her heart lurching. She shoved the shard of glass back into her pocket and pushed herself to her feet, ignoring the way her knees buckled beneath her. She grabbed the damp, bloodstained bandages and tucked them into her apron just as the door creaked open.

"Elysia?"

Vivienne stood in the doorway, her dark hair braided neatly over one shoulder, her nightdress covered by a silk wrapper embroidered with tiny glass roses. She looked almost ethereal in the soft light, though her expression was sharp with suspicion.

Elysia forced a smile, though it felt brittle. "Good morning, Vivienne."

Vivienne stepped inside, her gaze sweeping the small room with an assessing coolness that made Elysia's stomach twist. "Why are you awake?"

"I—" Elysia fumbled for words, her mind racing. "I woke early to start the fire in the kitchen hearth."

Vivienne's sharp gaze landed on Elysia's hands, which she quickly hid behind her back. "What's wrong with your hands?"

"Nothing."

"Don't lie to me," Vivienne snapped, her voice low. She stepped closer, her eyes narrowing. "You're hiding something. What is it?"

"I told you, it's nothing," Elysia said, her voice quiet but firm. She stepped back, keeping her bleeding hands out of view. "Please, Vivienne, I have work to do."

Vivienne studied her for a long moment, the silence stretching between them like a wire pulled taut. Elysia held her breath, her heart pounding painfully in her chest. Finally, Vivienne sniffed and turned away.

"Fine," she said coldly, walking toward the door. "But, Mother will hear about this if I catch you sneaking around again. I know you're up to something."

Elysia said nothing as Vivienne swept out of the room, the door clicking shut behind her. She waited, her body rigid, until the sound of footsteps faded down the hall.

Only then did she sink back onto the cot, burying her face in her hands.

Vivienne was growing suspicious. It was only a matter of time before she told Lady Seraphine—or worse, started following Elysia to uncover the truth herself. The thought sent ice through Elysia's veins. If anyone discovered the mirror, if they knew she was learning magic—forbidden magic—it would all be over.

She had to be careful. She couldn't let them see her falter.

With shaking hands, she reached under her pillow and pulled out the tiny object she had hidden there—a small, trembling, glass butterfly. It was imperfect, its wings cracked and uneven, but she had managed to salvage it before the rest shattered. It was proof. Proof that she had done it.

She held it up to the faint light, watching as it gleamed with a pale, fragile beauty.

Elysia stared at the butterfly, tears stinging the corners of her eyes. Her mother had always believed in things Elysia could not see—magic in the world, hope in the darkest places. But, that magic had never been meant for her.

Until now.

She closed her hand gently around the butterfly, careful not to break it. I will learn, she thought fiercely. I will control it. And, I will break this curse, no matter what it costs.

The hum of the glass echoed faintly in her memory, a promise that tugged at her bones.

Elysia curled up on the cot, cradling the butterfly in her palm as the first light of morning filled the room.

I won't fail again, she thought, her exhaustion pulling her under like a tide. Not this time.

The drawing room glittered in the morning light, alive with the sharp hum of glass magic. Sunbeams pierced the tall windows, catching on delicate glass roses that lined the mantle and floating ornaments that shimmered midair, spinning like captured stars. It was a room meant to dazzle—a place of beauty, wealth, and power.

It was also where Elysia was least wanted.

She stood at the edge of the room, broom in hand, trying to ignore the ache in her palms as she swept the marble floor. The cuts throbbed with every movement, but she couldn't stop. She dared not stop—not with Lady Seraphine's gaze so sharp and unrelenting as it drifted to her every so often.

Alessa lounged on the settee, twirling her fingers in lazy circles to keep a glass butterfly hovering above her lap. Its wings fluttered as though alive, glinting faintly gold where the light struck it. Across the room, Vivienne stood beside a low table, her brow furrowed in concentration as molten glass pooled in her palms. It moved like liquid silver, curling upward into the fragile shape of a rose.

"You're being sloppy," Lady Seraphine said, her cold voice breaking the silence. She stood near the windows, her hands clasped tightly at her waist as she watched Vivienne. "Your petals are uneven. Start over."

Vivienne bit her lip, her expression souring, but she let the rose collapse back into a molten pool with a sigh. Alessa smirked from her perch. "Sloppy? You? I thought precision was your talent, sister."

Vivienne shot her a glare, her hands glowing faintly as she began again. "Better sloppy than purposeless. How many butterflies have you made today? Five? Six? And they all look the same."

"Because they're perfect," Alessa said sweetly, flicking her wrist. The butterfly spun in a quick circle, its wings humming faintly before it flew toward Elysia.

Elysia froze, her grip on the broom tightening.

The butterfly hovered inches from her face, its edges so thin they looked like they might disappear. But, Elysia knew better. It was sharp. Everything they created with their magic was sharp.

"Don't you like it?" Alessa asked, her voice lilting with mock sweetness. "You should thank me. It's the closest you'll ever come to real magic."

Elysia said nothing, her jaw clenching as she looked away. She swept faster, forcing herself to focus on the rhythm of the broom against the marble: back and forth, back and forth.

The butterfly darted closer, skimming past her cheek. She flinched as its wing caught a stray lock of her hair, slicing through it like a knife.

"Enough, Alessa," Lady Seraphine said, though there was no sharpness to her tone—only a bored weariness. "You're wasting magic."

Alessa sighed dramatically, letting the butterfly flicker and fade. It dissolved into nothing, leaving the faintest hum in the air. "I was only having fun."

Vivienne straightened, holding up the new rose she had formed. This one was flawless—its petals smooth and thin, the shape so perfect it looked as though it might bloom. She turned to Lady Seraphine, seeking approval.

"Better," Lady Seraphine said with a nod. "Keep practicing."

Vivienne's gaze flicked toward Elysia, sharp and calculating. "Maybe Elysia should practice too," she said with a sly smile. "She could sweep with magic instead of a broom. Imagine that."

Alessa giggled. "Oh, don't be cruel. She'd probably drop the glass and bleed all over the floor. Again."

Elysia's hands trembled. The broom handle pressed against the raw cuts in her palms, each movement sending a fresh wave of pain up her arms. She swept harder, her breath coming quicker, her chest tight. Ignore them, she told herself. Ignore them.

"Elysia?" Vivienne's voice was soft and mocking. "Why are you shaking?"

"Enough." Lady Seraphine's voice cut across the room like a whip, making all three girls stiffen. "Stop this nonsense. You're wasting my time and yours."

"Yes, Mother," Alessa said with a sigh, slumping back onto the settee. Vivienne turned away with a small huff, but not before casting Elysia one last look—a look that lingered too long, sharp with suspicion.

Elysia's heartbeat roared in her ears. The air in the room felt heavy, pressing against her chest as though the walls themselves were closing in. She gripped the broom tighter, trying to steady her hands, trying to keep her breaths even.

They don't know, she told herself. They don't know what I've done. They can't.

But, the glass on the floor betrayed her.

It was faint at first—a low vibration that stirred at the

edges of her awareness. Then, it grew louder, sharper, until Elysia realized the shards of glass scattered at her feet trembled. The pieces from Vivienne's failed rose shifted against the marble, shivering as though caught in an unseen breeze.

Elysia froze.

No.

Her pulse quickened as panic clawed up her throat. She glanced at the others—Alessa, still lounging with her eyes closed, and Vivienne, watching her from across the room with narrowed eyes. Lady Seraphine's back was turned, her gaze fixed on the garden beyond the windows.

They haven't noticed.

Elysia squeezed her eyes shut, willing the glass to stop, to be still. She tried to shove the hum away, the strange, pulsing note she could feel deep in her chest, vibrating in her bones.

Be still. Please, be still.

The hum faltered. The glass stilled.

Elysia released a shaky breath, her grip on the broom loosening slightly. She forced herself to keep sweeping, though her knees felt weak, and the sweat at the back of her neck had turned cold.

Vivienne's voice broke the silence. "Why are you sweeping like that?"

Elysia looked up sharply. Vivienne was watching her, her gaze sharp, her head tilted slightly. "You look ill," she said. "Or guilty."

"I'm fine," Elysia said quickly, her voice steadier than she felt. "I'm just tired."

Vivienne didn't look convinced, but before she could

say anything more, Lady Seraphine turned back to the room. "Vivienne, enough."

"Yes, Mother," Vivienne said, though her gaze lingered on Elysia for a moment longer before she turned away.

Elysia swept the last of the glass into the dustpan, her hands still trembling. She could feel the blood seeping through the bandages again, soaking into her sleeves.

But as she straightened, the faint hum returned. The shards in the dustpan quivered, vibrating softly against the metal surface. Her pulse quickened. Not now, she thought desperately, clutching the dustpan tighter. She glanced over her shoulder, but Vivienne was still watching her, suspicion flickering in her sharp gaze.

"Why are you standing there?" Vivienne's voice sliced through the silence. "Didn't Mother tell you to clean faster?"

Elysia forced her trembling hands to move, tipping the shards into the waste bin. The hum faltered, fading just as Vivienne stepped closer. But, the other girl's eyes lingered on the faint smear of blood on Elysia's sleeve, her frown deepening.

"What are you hiding?" Vivienne demanded.

"Nothing," Elysia said quickly, backing away. Her heart thundered in her chest, the hum still ringing faintly in her ears. She couldn't let Vivienne get closer—not when the glass might betray her at any moment.

Once in the hallway, she sagged against the wall, her breath shaking as she pressed her bleeding palms against her apron. The house was quiet here, the drawing room's hum of magic fading behind her.

But, her mind raced, the echo of the glass's hum ringing in her ears.

It had responded to her. She hadn't even meant to call it, and it had moved.

You're losing control, Caius's voice whispered in her memory. Glass doesn't forgive weakness.

Elysia stared at the faint smear of blood on her apron, the sharp pain in her hands grounding her. She couldn't let it happen again. She couldn't slip, not in front of them.

She pushed away from the wall and hurried toward the kitchen, her footsteps echoing faintly in the empty hall. She had to be careful now.

Because if Vivienne noticed again—if anyone noticed —there would be no hiding what she'd done.

CHAPTER 4

THE BALL AND THE WARNING

The dining room glittered with morning light, as though the sun itself bowed to the glass brilliance of Lady Seraphine's house. The tall windows cast slants of gold across the long table, where Alessa and Vivienne sat like queens draped in silk. Glass dishes caught the light, throwing flecks of rainbows onto the walls and ceiling. Even the cutlery gleamed with magic—silver and glass merged so seamlessly it might have been spun from light itself.

And in the shadows, Elysia stood.

She kept her hands folded on her apron as she waited. Her shoulders hunched as she poured steaming tea into Alessa's glass cup. The smooth surface trembled faintly in her grip, but the stepsisters didn't notice. They never did.

"Careful, Elysia," Vivienne said lazily, breaking the silence. "If you shatter that, Mother will make you pay for it."

"Don't tease her, Vivienne," Alessa replied, smirking

faintly. "It's not her fault. Can you imagine having hands so clumsy? I'd never recover."

Elysia said nothing, her face blank as she returned the teapot to its stand. She was used to their mockery, the way their words cut sharper than any glass blade. But today, their laughter buzzed at the edges of her mind, muted by the exhaustion still clinging to her bones.

She gripped the edge of the table to steady herself as Lady Seraphine entered the room. The air seemed to shift with her arrival. Lady Seraphine's gown swept the floor in waves of emerald silk, her glass hairpins catching every sliver of light and refracting it into gleaming spears. Her presence turned the sunlight cruel.

Elysia lowered her gaze as Lady Seraphine took her seat at the head of the table. "Girls," she said, her voice cutting through the room like ice, "enough chattering. There's something we must discuss."

Vivienne straightened in her chair, her fingers falling still around her spoon. Alessa raised an eyebrow, looking momentarily interested.

Lady Seraphine snapped her fingers. From the center of the table, the royal seal appeared—a small, floating crystal etched with the king's insignia. Elysia's breath caught as the crystal began to hum softly, its glow spreading outward until a scroll of paper formed beneath it, suspended midair. The scroll unfurled with a flourish, and the voice of the royal herald filled the room, deep and resonant.

"By decree of His Majesty, King Edric of Solmaris, all families of noble rank are summoned to attend a grand ball at the royal palace three nights hence. The event shall honor His Highness, Prince Rilian, who shall soon choose his bride among the worthy families of this realm."

Vivienne gasped, her spoon clattering onto her plate. "The prince? Our prince?"

Alessa's eyes widened, and for the first time that morning, Elysia saw something real flicker across her face: ambition. "He's choosing a bride? At the ball?"

The scroll continued, the herald's voice growing louder as though to emphasize the importance of his words.

"It is His Majesty's will that all noble families display their finest glass magics at this gathering. Let beauty and power be a tribute to the kingdom, and let the most worthy be seen."

The scroll snapped closed and dissolved into a flurry of shimmering light. The royal crystal vanished, leaving the room silent, except for the faint hum of magic lingering in the air.

Vivienne was the first to break it, her voice breathless. "Mother, we must prepare! This is our chance—our chance to stand before the prince!"

Alessa turned to Lady Seraphine, eyes alight with excitement. "Imagine how the court will admire us—our roses, our butterflies. We'll dazzle them all!"

Lady Seraphine smiled faintly, though the look in her eyes was calculating. "Indeed," she said, her tone cool. "The two of you will be the finest in attendance. There will be no flaw in your magic, no imperfection in your presentation. Do you understand me?"

"Yes, Mother," Vivienne and Alessa said in unison, their voices eager.

Elysia stood frozen at the table's edge, her fingers

curling tighter against the cloth of her apron. A ball. The prince.

Her heart thudded in her chest, the thought surging wildly in her mind. Could he lift it? The curse that bound her family, the emptiness that had defined her for as long as she could remember—what if he could change it? Kings and princes could lift curses, could they not? They were woven from magic itself, their bloodlines steeped in power.

The thought burned brightly, too brightly. Her fingers curled tighter against the fabric, and a faint vibration stirred in the air. She froze. The glass centerpiece on the dining table, a delicate sculpture of interwoven roses, began to tremble.

Lady Seraphine's sharp gaze turned toward the glass, her lips pressing into a thin line. "What is that?" she said, her voice cold and precise, like the edge of a blade.

Vivienne frowned, her eyes darted toward the glass sculpture. It quivered faintly, as though alive and restless under the weight of her thoughts. "Is it enchanted?"

"No," Alessa replied, a faint edge of irritation in her voice. "It's stable."

Elysia forced herself to steady her breathing, willing the glass to still. Her thoughts raced. Stop. Stop it. But, the hum only grew louder, the roses vibrating faintly against their crystal base.

Lady Seraphine's gaze snapped to Elysia, her eyes narrowing. "Elysia."

Her name was a lash, and she flinched under it. "Yes, Stepmother?" she said quickly, lowering her head.

"Go to the kitchen. Now."

"Yes, Stepmother," Elysia murmured, her voice tight as

she turned away. The glass steadied as she left the room, but her stepsisters' laughter trailed after her.

Behind her, Alessa's voice rang out like a bell. "She probably thinks she'll be going, too."

Vivienne laughed. "Poor Elysia. You're not worthy of an invitation, are you? Perhaps they'll let you sweep the palace steps. That would suit you."

Their laughter followed her down the hall, each note sharp and grating.

The kitchen was dark and cool when Elysia stepped inside, the scent of ashes and soap grounding her as she leaned heavily against the wall. She pressed her hands to her chest, her heartbeat hammering beneath her ribs.

Could it be possible? she wondered again. Could the ball be a chance to escape this life, to reclaim the magic that had been stolen from her family? The very thought sent a shiver through her—half hope, half terror.

But Caius's voice whispered in her mind, cold and sharp as a blade. "Power does not save you, Elysia. It destroys you."

Elysia swallowed hard, pushing the memory aside.

Her gaze fell to her hands—her fingers stiff with scars, the faint cuts on her palms aching with every movement. Her stepfamily would dazzle the court with roses and butterflies, with power that spun beauty from air. But, Elysia had her own magic now—untrained, dangerous, and alive.

I will go, she thought fiercely, the idea taking root in

her heart like a spark catching kindling. I will go, and I will be seen.

But not as herself.

Her reflection stared back at her from the smudged kitchen window, faint and flickering in the dim light. She leaned closer, studying the face that looked out at her: pale, hollow-eyed, a girl draped in ash and shadows. This was who they saw. This was who she had always been.

Her gaze dropped to her hands—scarred, raw, still faintly trembling from the night's work. What would the prince see? What would the court see? Certainly not a bride. Certainly not a girl worthy of magic or power.

She thought of masks—the kind her stepmother might wear to court, glittering with glass and sharp with beauty. Would one of those make her less of a shadow? Would it hide the truth of her?

A bitter laugh rose unbidden to her throat. The mask would only replace one lie with another. It would not change the hollow girl behind it. And yet... perhaps the lie was enough. Perhaps the lie was all she needed.

Night draped the house in shadow by the time Elysia slipped out the back door, her apron tied tightly around her waist, her steps soundless on the frost-covered ground. The garden was silent, the moon hanging low in the sky, casting everything in silver. The shed loomed ahead, its crooked outline darker than the night itself.

She hesitated at the door, her breath misting in the cold air. The mirror was inside—waiting. Watching. She had dragged it here days ago, but every time she returned, she felt its pull a little more keenly, as though it were alive.

Because it is alive, she thought. Or rather, Caius was. And tonight, she needed answers.

With a trembling hand, Elysia pushed open the door. The hinges groaned, loud enough to make her wince, and she slipped inside, closing the door behind her. The air was thick with the scent of earth and forgotten things. Her candle's small flame flickered, barely holding back the dark.

Against the wall, the mirror sat where she had left it. Its silver frame gleamed faintly in the candlelight, the curling vines etched into the surface twisting like frozen shadows. The glass itself was black—so dark it seemed to drink the light, smooth and deep as still water.

And then, it rippled.

Caius's face emerged from the darkness, his black eyes gleaming faintly as they settled on her. He looked sharper tonight—his edges more defined, as though the shadows themselves had carved him into focus. His lips curled faintly in what might have been a smile, though there was nothing warm about it.

"Back so soon, little cinder-girl?" His voice slithered through the room, soft and low, curling around her like smoke. "Have you come to tell me you've given up?"

"No," Elysia said, standing taller despite the chill gnawing at her spine. "I need to ask you something."

Caius arched an eyebrow. "Do you, now? How curious. Most people don't ask mirrors for advice."

"There's going to be a ball," she said quickly, ignoring

his jibe. "At the palace. The prince will be there. He's looking for a bride."

Caius's expression didn't change, but something flickered behind his eyes—something sharp and wary. "A ball."

"Yes," she pressed, stepping closer. "The court will be there. The nobility. If I could speak to the prince—"

"No." The word was a whipcrack, and Elysia froze. Caius leaned forward, his face filling the glass. "Forget the ball, Elysia." His tone darkened, the sharp edge of warning slicing through his words.

"Forget the prince." He leaned forward, his black eyes narrowing. "Do you know what happens to glass under too much pressure? It fractures. The court would grind you into shards and scatter you to the wind." His voice softened, but it lost none of its menace. "But perhaps that's what you want—a thousand pieces scattered, so no one can see who you really are."

She blinked, the heat of her resolve flickering under the weight of his voice. "But—"

"You think the court will save you?" Caius's voice turned sharper, the edges of his reflection rippling like water disturbed. "Do you think princes break curses because it pleases them? The court does not offer salvation. It offers chains."

Elysia frowned. "The royal family is powerful. If anyone can help me—"

Caius laughed, though there was no humor in it. It was a cold, brittle sound, like glass breaking. "The royal family would sooner kill you than help you."

Elysia stared at him, her chest tight. "Why?"

Caius's gaze pinned her in place, his black eyes

gleaming with something dark and dangerous. "Because the court does not suffer threats. Do you think your magic is harmless? Do you think they would look at you—at what you are—and see anything but a criminal?"

Her throat tightened. "I haven't done anything wrong."

"Not yet," Caius said softly, his voice curling like smoke. "But you will."

Elysia flinched, the words striking a nerve. "I don't care what they think. If the prince can help me—"

"The prince cannot help you." Caius's voice was low, but it shook the air. The candle flame shuddered, shrinking to a thin, flickering thread of light. "The prince is nothing but a pawn wrapped in silk. He wears a crown, yes—but it is glass. It will cut him as surely as it will cut you."

Elysia hesitated, the weight of his words pressing against her resolve. She didn't want to believe him. She couldn't.

"Why are you so afraid of them?" she whispered. "What did they do to you?"

For the first time, Caius stilled. The glass surface went dark around him, the edges of his face blurring as though the mirror were swallowing him whole. When he spoke again, his voice was softer, almost distant.

"I was not always here," he said. "Once, I stood in the court you speak of so fondly. I wielded magic that could shape the world. I was a master of glass."

Elysia stared at him, her pulse quickening. "And then?"

"And then, they turned on me." His black eyes met hers again, sharper now, gleaming like shards of obsidian.

"Power is not a gift, Elysia. It is a threat. They will take it from you. They will take everything from you."

The room was silent. The candle flame trembled, its faint light barely holding back the shadows that pressed close around her.

Elysia swallowed hard, but she didn't look away. "I don't have a choice. This curse—my family's curse—I need to break it. If the prince can't help me, then I'll find another way. But, I will go to that ball."

Caius's lips curled into a smile, slow and cold. "So determined. You remind me of someone."

"Who?"

"Someone who reached for power they couldn't control."

Elysia frowned, but before she could ask more, Caius leaned back, his reflection fading slightly as though the mirror itself were drawing him away. "If you insist on going to the court, you must be careful."

"How?"

His gaze locked onto hers, black and unblinking. "Wear a mask, little cinder-girl. Hide your power. Hide yourself. They cannot destroy what they do not see."

Elysia nodded, though her heart pounded in her chest. She stepped back from the mirror, her fingers brushing against her apron as she turned the words over in her mind.

Caius's voice followed her as she moved to leave. "And remember this, Elysia—glass reflects. Be careful what you show it."

The words hung in the air, heavy and cold, as she stepped into the night.

Elysia sat on the edge of her narrow cot, the darkness pressing in close around her. The moon hung low outside the window, its pale light filtering through the cracks in the shutters and falling in faint streaks across the stone floor. The air in the room felt heavy, thick with dust and silence.

Her fingers brushed against the glass shard in her lap. It was the last piece of the butterfly she had tried to save— a fragile, fractured thing, its edges uneven and sharp. She held it up to the faint light, staring into its fractured surface.

Her own reflection stared back at her, splintered and distorted.

"Glass reflects," Caius's voice echoed in her mind, soft and cold. "Be careful what you show it."

Elysia closed her eyes, pressing her thumb against the shard's sharp edge until it bit into her skin. She thought of Caius's warnings—his voice sharp with bitterness, the way the shadows had convulsed behind him like something alive. The court will destroy you. The prince will not save you.

But, his words had come too late. The idea of the ball had already taken root inside her, a spark too bright to be snuffed out.

Her family's curse had stolen everything from them— magic, status, worth. She had lived her entire life in the empty shell of a house that once held greatness, reduced to cleaning the ashes of other people's power. It was her

61

family's name that was spat on, her empty hands that were mocked.

She was tired of it.

Elysia opened her eyes, her resolve hardening like iron beneath her ribs. "I'll go," she whispered to the glass shard, as though the words themselves might make it true. "I don't care what he says. I'll go to the ball."

Her reflection stared back at her, fractured but unbroken.

The risks clawed at her mind, whispering of ruin, of Lady Seraphine's wrath, of the gallows where criminals hung for breaking the king's laws. Caius was right about one thing: power was not a gift—it was a threat. And forbidden magic could get her killed.

But, the curse was killing her already. Slowly. Quietly.

She remembered the royal decree—the way the scroll had floated midair, its words booming with magic and power. Let beauty and power be a tribute to the kingdom, and let the most worthy be seen.

The most worthy.

What would it take for her to be seen?

Her hand closed around the shard, the edges biting into her palm. She thought of Vivienne's roses, flawless and cold. Of Alessa's butterflies, spinning midair like living light. They would walk into the palace as though they belonged there, draped in silks and cloaked in magic, while she swept the ashes they left behind.

Not this time.

She could not attend the ball as herself. Lady Seraphine would never allow it, and her stepsisters would claw her apart before she reached the gates. But, she didn't need to be herself. She needed to be someone else—someone invisible, untouchable.

"Wear a mask," Caius had said. "They cannot destroy what they do not see."

Elysia rose from the bed, her legs unsteady beneath her. The room swayed faintly, exhaustion gnawing at the edges of her vision, but she pushed it aside. Her fingers fumbled through the chest at the foot of her cot, pulling out the remnants of her mother's things—a faded cloak, threadbare and patched, and an old pair of gloves with holes worn through the fingertips.

She held the cloak up to the light. Once, it had been beautiful. Now, its fabric was worn and dull, its color long faded to the gray of forgotten things. It would not do.

But, I can fix it, she thought, the spark of an idea flaring in her mind. Her gaze drifted to the window, to the faint glow of the moon beyond the shutters. She had glass magic now—untrained and dangerous, yes, but alive. She could feel it humming faintly beneath her skin, as though it had been waiting for her to call it.

She would make herself a dress. A cloak. A mask. Something to hide behind, something that would let her slip into the court unseen.

The thought sent a shiver through her.

Is this what you want, Elysia? the doubt whispered. To play with fire until it burns you alive?

She thought of Alessa's laughter, of Vivienne's sharp gaze and Lady Seraphine's voice, cold and cruel: You are nothing. You will always be nothing.

Her hands curled into fists, the shard of glass digging

into her skin again. "No," she said aloud, the word soft but steady. "Not anymore."

She crossed the room to the window, pressing her palm against the cool glass. Outside, the night stretched on, vast and quiet. The palace lay far beyond the horizon, a place she had only seen in glimpses, its glass spires gleaming like fire in the sunlight.

A ball awaited her there—a room full of magic and power, of kings and princes, of opportunity and danger. It was a risk that could cost her everything.

But, it was also the only chance she had.

Elysia pulled the glass shard from her pocket and turned it over in her hands. Slowly, carefully, she whispered the word Caius had taught her during one of their secret lessons—a word he'd described as the key to awakening the magic slumbering within the glass.

The first time he'd said it, the word had felt like a distant melody, strange and ancient. "It's not just a sound," he'd warned, his voice sharp with caution. "It's a command. Speak it with intention, or the glass will resist you."

Now, as she whispered it, the shard trembled faintly in her palm, humming as though answering her call. The sound was faint at first, like the stirrings of a harp string, but it grew louder, warmer. She stared at the shard, feeling the weight of the moment settle deep in her chest.

"If I must go," she whispered, holding the shard up to the moonlight, "I'll go as someone they cannot see."

The shard gleamed, sharp and beautiful, the light splitting across its fractured surface like a promise.

CHAPTER 5

FORGING THE MASK

E lysia shivered with cold as she stepped inside the garden shed, the kind of cold that settled in the bones and refused to let go, her candle flickering wildly in the draft. She closed the door behind her, sealing herself into the darkness, the hum of the night settling heavy on her shoulders.

Against the far wall, the mirror awaited her, its surface dark and still as a frozen pond. The silver frame gleamed faintly in the candlelight, its edges twisting like thorned vines, the details impossibly intricate—too alive for something so old and dead.

Elysia hesitated, her hand hovering over the cloth that usually hid the glass. Why are you doing this? the doubt whispered. But, she pushed it aside and tugged the cloth free.

The mirror's surface shivered outward like water disturbed. From the depths of the dark glass, Caius's face appeared, as though he'd been waiting for her. His black eyes fixed on her immediately, sharp and glinting, and the faintest trace of a smile curled his lips.

"Back again, little cinder-girl?" he purred, his voice soft and mocking. "I was beginning to think you'd finally seen sense and abandoned this foolishness."

Elysia swallowed, her hands trembling as she set the candle down on the dusty workbench. The flame shuddered, its light weak against the shadows that gathered around the mirror.

"I need your help," she said. Her voice came out steadier than she felt.

Caius's smile widened. "Oh, this promises to be entertaining. What kind of help, exactly?" His gaze sharpened. "Not another butterfly, I hope. I'd rather not waste my time."

Elysia took a breath, squaring her shoulders. "I want to craft something bigger. A mask. And a gown."

For the first time, Caius's expression faltered. The shadows behind him seemed to ebb and swell, dark waves lapping at the edges of his reflection.

"A mask?" His voice was soft, dangerous. "And a gown? Made of glass?"

"Yes." She didn't blink. "I need them for the royal ball."

Caius's gaze sharpened, his dark eyes narrowing like a predator assessing reckless prey. "You can't be serious."

"I am."

Caius's laughter burst out, sharp and brittle, echoing in the small space like shattering glass. It wasn't the laughter of someone amused—it was cruel, full of disdain. "You would drape yourself in glass? In something you can barely control? Do you think this is a game?"

"I've practiced," Elysia said, lifting her chin. "I reinforced the gown with patterns of tempered enchantments. It's stable, it will hold." She hesitated, her voice dipping lower. "The mask... is more delicate."

"Delicate?" Caius leaned forward, his reflection rippling in the glass. "It's a liability. Do you have any idea what will happen if it fractures in front of them?"

"I know." Her voice wavered, but only for a moment. "I'll keep it together. I have to."

The silence stretched between them, cold and thick, until Caius finally spoke again, his voice low and flat. "Foolish," he muttered, more to himself than to her. "But perhaps you'll learn your lesson the hard way."

Elysia swallowed hard, her hand trembling briefly before she steadied it. Foolish or not, she had no other choice.

"It's not a game," Elysia said fiercely, her voice rising. "You said glass obeys strength and will. I can do this."

Caius's laughter died abruptly. His face turned cold as stone, his eyes narrowing. "What you're asking for is beyond anything you understand. Do you know how fragile glass is? How easily it breaks?" He leaned closer, his reflection expanding as though the mirror itself was pushing him toward her. "Do you know what it means to fail when the magic is in your hands?"

Elysia's mouth went dry, but she didn't look away. "I know the risks. But, I need to do this."

"Why?" Caius demanded, his voice like a whip. "To impress some spoiled prince? To parade before the court in pretty shards?"

"No." The word came out hard, a knife wrapped in silk. "Because it's my only chance."

Caius stilled, his expression unreadable. For a long moment, he simply watched her, the glass around his face fluttering as though breathing.

Elysia pressed on, her voice quiet but unyielding. "If I go to the ball, maybe I can find a way to break my family's curse. Maybe the prince can help me, or maybe I'll find another way. I don't know yet." Her fists tightened at her sides. "But, I can't do it like this. I can't go as myself."

Caius tilted his head, his gaze never leaving her. "So, you would wear a mask," he said softly. "Hide yourself behind glass and shadows."

"Yes."

"And, if it shatters?"

"Then, I'll pick up the pieces," she said quietly.

The corners of Caius's mouth lifted, though it wasn't quite a smile. "Such determination," he murmured. "You're beginning to sound like me."

The words sent a chill down her spine, but she refused to let it show. "Will you help me or not?"

Caius's expression shifted, his gaze calculating as though he were weighing her against something unseen. At last, he sighed, leaning back into the shadows of the mirror. "Fine. If you insist on hurling yourself off this particular cliff, who am I to stop you?"

Relief flooded Elysia's chest, but it was short-lived as Caius continued, his voice turning sharp. "Listen to me carefully, little cinder-girl. What you're asking isn't a game. Shaping glass like this will demand everything from you—your focus, your strength, your very will. If your mind falters for even a moment, the magic will splinter, and you'll be lucky if all it takes is your blood."

"I understand," Elysia said softly.

Caius's black eyes bored into hers. "No, you don't. Not yet. But you will."

The mirror wavered again as Caius shifted, as though he were moving deeper into its shadows. When he spoke again, his voice was low, almost a whisper. "We begin with the mask. Smaller, simpler—if you can even manage that."

Elysia nodded, her hands trembling. She reached into her apron and pulled out a small shard of glass she had taken earlier—a piece as thin and sharp as a thorn. She held it up for Caius to see.

"Good," he murmured, his tone clipped and watchful. "Sit. Focus. You know the hum, don't you?"

"Yes," she whispered.

"Then listen for it." His voice dropped lower, curling through the darkness like smoke. "Let the glass hear you. See the mask in your mind. Shape it—command it. Do not stop until it obeys."

The candle was nearly spent, its tiny flame flickering low as Elysia sat cross-legged on the cold, dirt floor of the garden shed. The glass shard rested in her palm, smooth and deceptively innocent. But it was alive now—she could feel it hum faintly beneath her fingertips, as though waiting for her to act.

In the mirror, Caius watched her like a predator, his sharp eyes narrowed with expectation. The shadows behind him seemed to coil and writhe, mirroring her own fear.

"Focus," he said, his voice low and sharp. "You've already shaped glass before, Elysia. This is no different. Listen to the hum. Command it."

Elysia swallowed, her throat dry, her pulse thudding like a drum in her ears. She had held the magic once—just enough to coax the glass into a shape. But this was different. This was more. A mask was not a butterfly or a thread; it was something with edges, curves, and intention. It needed to be beautiful. It needed to be perfect.

She didn't know if she was strong enough to make it.

"Breathe," Caius snapped, breaking through her hesitation. "If you doubt yourself, the glass will doubt you. And it will shatter."

Elysia clenched her jaw, steadying her hands as she closed her eyes. The air in the shed pressed against her skin like frost. The glass shard in her palm vibrated softly, the hum building just beneath her awareness, like a sound she could almost hear.

She let out a slow breath and reached for it, her mind focusing on the image she'd been holding onto since last night.

A mask. Thin, smooth, delicate as frost on a windowpane. Its edges would be sharp and perfect, but its surface would gleam like moonlight—something a queen might wear, something that would let her disappear into a room of silk and glass.

The hum swelled, and the warmth bloomed in her chest, spreading down her arms like fire threading through her veins. The shard trembled in her palm, alive and restless, as though it were waiting for her command.

Shape it, she thought fiercely. Make it.

"Good," Caius murmured, his voice curling around her like smoke. "Now hold that image. Do not let it falter."

The hum grew louder, the shard growing hotter, until it felt as though it might burn through her skin. Elysia's hands shook with the effort, but she didn't let go. The image of the mask remained sharp in her mind, her will pouring into it like molten gold.

She opened her eyes, gasping softly.

The shard had begun to change.

It lifted from her palm, the edges unraveling like threads of liquid light. They twisted and reformed midair, curling upward as though following the shape she held in her mind. Elysia watched in awe as the mask took form, piece by fragile piece. It gleamed faintly in the candlelight, its surface smooth and impossibly thin, like it might vanish if she blinked.

It's working, she thought, her chest tightening with something like joy.

But then, her focus wavered. For the briefest moment, she saw herself reflected in the surface of the half-formed mask—her pale face, her wide, tired eyes—and the hum faltered.

The glass convulsed violently.

"No!" Caius's voice cracked like a whip. "Focus! Hold it!"

Elysia gritted her teeth, sweat gathering at the back of her neck as she forced the image back into place. The glass trembled, the humming note rising to a frantic pitch, but she held on, pouring every ounce of her will into the mask.

Her arms shook. Her palms burned.

And then, as suddenly as it had started, the hum stopped.

The mask fell into her hands, solid and cool, the glass humming faintly with an energy she could still feel thrumming through her bones. Elysia stared down at it, her breath coming in shallow gasps.

It was beautiful.

The mask was thin and light, its edges sharp but perfectly curved to fit the contours of a face. It gleamed faintly, like frost caught in moonlight, and for one moment, Elysia forgot to breathe.

But then, she saw it.

A crack—thin as a hairline—ran through the mask's left side, splitting across the cheekbone and down to the edge. It was almost invisible, but it was there. A single flaw.

Elysia's heart sank.

"It's cracked," she whispered, turning it over in her trembling hands.

Caius tilted his head, his black eyes glinting faintly. "Of course, it's cracked. What did you expect?"

Elysia looked up sharply. "But, I did everything you said—"

"And still, you wavered," Caius interrupted coldly. "Glass does not forgive weakness, Elysia. Even a moment's hesitation will leave its mark."

Elysia looked back down at the mask, her fingers brushing over the crack. It was sharp beneath her touch, a jagged scar against the otherwise flawless surface. I wavered, she thought bitterly. Because I saw myself.

"What do I do now?" she murmured.

"You wear it," Caius said simply. "Imperfection is not failure. You wanted a mask, and now you have one."

"But, it's not perfect," she said, her voice soft.

Caius laughed softly, a sound that sent a chill through her bones. "Nothing is ever perfect, little cinder-girl. Not masks. Not glass. Not you."

Elysia flinched, his words hitting her like a blade.

"Take it and go," Caius said, his voice turning bored as his reflection began to darken. "If you want perfection, you'll have to earn it."

The mirror stilled, the shadows swallowing Caius's face until only her reflection remained, dim and fractured.

Elysia sat in silence, the mask resting in her lap. She traced the crack with her fingertip, her chest aching. She had done it—she had shaped glass magic into something real, something hers. But, the crack felt like a reflection of herself: flawed, fragile, and on the verge of breaking.

It's enough, she told herself. She picked up the mask, holding it carefully in her hands as though it might shatter with the wrong touch. It has to be enough.

She rose to her feet, her legs unsteady beneath her, and carefully wrapped the mask in a strip of cloth. The glass was cool and quiet now, its hum faded to a whisper.

Elysia turned back to the mirror one last time. Her reflection stared back at her, pale and hollow-eyed, but the mask lay hidden in her hands, a promise of what she could become.

I will wear this, she thought, her resolve hardening like iron. They will see me.

She blew out the candle, plunging the shed into darkness.

The house was deathly silent when Elysia slipped back inside. The heavy front door closed behind her with the faintest groan of hinges, and she stilled, holding her breath. For a moment, the only sound was the pounding of her own heartbeat, echoing in her ears like the hum of the glass she had just shaped.

Her steps were slow, careful as she moved through the darkened corridors, her arms wrapped tightly around the small bundle in her hands. The mask lay hidden beneath layers of cloth, shielded from sight—but not from her thoughts. Its presence was a weight against her ribs, equal parts triumph and dread.

It's enough, she told herself again. It's enough to be seen.

A whisper of doubt slithered through her mind, faint as smoke. What if it's not?

The thought gnawed at her as she climbed the narrow staircase leading to her room. The wood creaked faintly beneath her feet, each sound a dagger of panic. If Lady Seraphine or her stepsisters found her awake at this hour —if they found the mask—it would all be over before it began.

When she reached her room, Elysia slipped inside and closed the door behind her with shaking hands. She sagged against it, her forehead resting against the cold wood as the breath shuddered from her lungs. For a moment, she let herself stay there, the weight of the night settling over her like a leaden cloak.

Her body ached. Her arms trembled with exhaustion, and the burns on her palms throbbed like open wounds, faint trails of blood seeping through her bandages. Glass magic was not kind. It was not forgiving.

And yet, despite everything—despite the cuts and the burns and the crack in the mask—she had done it.

Elysia pushed herself upright and crossed to her cot, lighting a small stub of a candle with trembling hands. The flame sputtered and glowed, casting soft light across the room—enough to reveal the bare walls, the crooked shutters, and the small chest of forgotten things at the foot of her bed.

She sat down carefully on the edge of the cot, placing the bundle in her lap. Slowly, she unwrapped the cloth, her fingers catching on the rough fabric as she pulled it away.

The mask lay nestled at the center, a fragile thing of pale glass. Even by candlelight, it gleamed softly, as though it held the moon itself within its surface. Its edges were sharp, its curves delicate. And yet...

Her gaze traced the crack that split down one side, running like a jagged scar across its smooth surface. It was almost invisible—so faint that someone might not notice, unless they looked closely. But, Elysia saw it. She couldn't not see it.

She lifted the mask carefully, holding it up to the candlelight. It cast faint reflections across the walls, fractured and shimmering, like pieces of a dream.

Is this enough? she wondered, her fingers brushing over the crack. It was a mask, yes—but it wasn't perfect. It would hide her face, but what if the glass broke? What if someone saw through it?

Caius's voice echoed in her mind, sharp and cruel. "Glass does not forgive imperfection."

Elysia closed her eyes, her shoulders sagging as exhaustion pulled at her limbs. Her hands throbbed where the glass had bitten into her skin, but it was nothing compared to the ache in her chest—a deep, gnawing weight that refused to leave her.

She thought of Lady Seraphine's voice, cold and cutting. "You are nothing."

She thought of Alessa and Vivienne, their cruel laughter like shards of ice. "You'll never be worthy."

And then, she thought of the royal ball—the glittering court, the prince who would choose a bride, the nobility displaying their glass magic as though it were spun from starlight. They would look right past her, as they always did.

Unless I make them see me.

Elysia opened her eyes. The mask gleamed in her hands, its crack faint but visible—a flaw that felt almost alive. She stared at it for a long moment before wrapping it carefully back in the cloth. It wasn't perfect. Neither was she.

But it would do.

She rose to her feet, wincing as the effort sent pain shooting through her arms, and crossed to the small chest at the foot of her bed. Opening the lid, she placed the bundle carefully inside, tucking it beneath the faded cloak she had taken from her mother's things. The mask would remain there, hidden, until she needed it.

Elysia straightened, her hands hovering over the chest as though she might pull the mask back out again. She didn't. Instead, she closed the lid and turned away, the flickering candlelight casting her shadow long and thin against the stone wall.

She moved to the basin in the corner of the room, where a small pitcher of water sat waiting. Her fingers fumbled as she poured it into the bowl, the water splashing faintly against the porcelain. It was ice cold as she dipped her hands in, her breath catching as the cuts along her palms screamed in protest.

She scrubbed them clean, watching as the water turned faintly pink. The blood swirled like ribbons before vanishing down the drain, leaving only her raw, trembling hands behind.

When she lifted her head, her gaze caught on the cracked mirror that hung above the basin. Her reflection stared back at her—pale skin smudged with ash, hair falling loose around her face, dark circles hollowing her eyes.

She looked fragile. Small.

But, she wasn't. Not anymore.

"I'll go," she whispered to the mirror, her voice soft but steady. The reflection of her lips moved with hers, though the girl staring back seemed to wear a different expression —one sharper, harder. "I'll wear the mask, and I'll be seen."

The candle flickered suddenly, the flame dancing wildly before settling again. For a moment, Elysia thought she saw something else in the mirror—a shadow behind her reflection, faint and formless, like a whisper of smoke.

She blinked, and it was gone.

Elysia turned away from the mirror and crossed to her cot, extinguishing the candle with a pinch of her fingers. The room plunged into darkness, save for the faint glow of moonlight seeping through the shutters.

She lay down slowly, the ache in her body settling deeper as she pulled the thin blanket over her shoulders. Sleep pulled at her like a tide, but her mind wouldn't rest. Instead, it turned over the events of the night—the mask, Caius's warnings, the crack that marred her creation.

It didn't matter.

The mask was made. The ball was coming.

And for the first time in her life, Elysia wouldn't hide in the shadows.

CHAPTER 6
A DANGEROUS GAME

The drawing room was alive with light and sound. Sunlight streamed through the tall windows, casting warm golden beams across the floor and setting the glass creations within the room ablaze. Rainbows glimmered on the walls and ceiling, reflections caught from butterflies of glass that fluttered aimlessly in the air, their delicate wings humming faintly.

Elysia stood at the edge of the room, broom in hand, watching silently as her stepsisters prepared for the royal ball.

Alessa reclined on a velvet-backed chaise, her fingers flicking lazily as she sent her glass butterflies spinning and diving through the air like living things. Each one was perfect—thin, translucent, and etched with faint patterns that shimmered when they caught the light. They looked so delicate, so impossibly beautiful, that for a moment Elysia almost forgot how sharp their edges must be.

"Higher," Alessa murmured, a note of satisfaction in her voice as she sent one of the butterflies soaring to the ceiling. It hovered there, its wings catching the sun before it drifted lazily back to the ground. "Imagine when the prince sees them. He won't look at anyone else."

Across the room, Vivienne sat straight-backed at a small table, her gaze fixed on the molten glass she cupped in her hands. It glowed faintly silver as it swirled and shifted, reshaping itself beneath her fingers into the form of another perfect rose.

"That's because he won't have to," Vivienne replied without looking up. "When he sees my roses—" She held up the glass flower she had just formed, its petals thin and flawless, curving inward in exquisite spirals. "—he'll know there's no one better."

"You've made dozens of those already," Alessa said with a sniff, waving her hand to send a butterfly darting dangerously close to her sister's head. "At least my butterflies have movement. Roses are so... still."

Vivienne set the rose carefully on the table beside its identical twins and glared at Alessa. "Movement won't impress him when everyone else can conjure the same tired tricks."

Elysia swept quietly along the far edge of the room, keeping her head down, her hands wrapped tightly around the broom handle. Her stepsisters didn't look at her—they never did when they were like this, so absorbed in their own beauty and ambition that they could see nothing else.

Lady Seraphine stood near the windows, her sharp gaze sweeping across the room like a hawk's. She wore a gown of deep emerald, the color so dark it swallowed the sunlight, and her hair was twisted into an intricate braid, pinned with gleaming shards of green glass. Her presence filled the room, heavy and suffocating.

She watched Alessa and Vivienne with a critical eye, her lips pressed into a thin line. "It's not enough," she said suddenly, breaking the tense silence.

Alessa's butterfly faltered midair, dipping sharply before regaining its height. Vivienne's fingers stilled around the rose she had begun shaping. Both girls turned to their mother in confusion.

"Mother?" Vivienne asked, her voice tight.

Lady Seraphine's gaze sharpened. "You heard me. These... decorations are charming, yes, but they are not extraordinary. You are competing for the attention of the prince. Do you think glass butterflies and roses will be enough to outshine the other noble families?"

"We're the best," Alessa said quickly, her eyes narrowing. "No one else can—"

"No one else will care," Lady Seraphine cut in coldly. "What you bring to the ball must be flawless, yes, but it must also be unexpected. Memorable. A true display of power."

Vivienne straightened, her shoulders rigid. "Then, I'll make something better."

"So will I," Alessa added, though her voice wavered slightly.

Lady Seraphine inclined her head, though her expression remained hard. "Good. You will start again tomorrow. I want perfection."

Elysia lowered her gaze as she swept closer to the table where Vivienne's roses sat gleaming. There were so many of them—so many perfect, beautiful things. The table was covered in glass petals, each one catching the sunlight, each one impossibly smooth and flawless.

It made Elysia's hands ache to look at them.

Her broom caught on something—a glass shard, sharp and jagged, that had fallen beneath the table. She winced as she bent to pick it up, careful not to let it bite into her bandaged fingers.

"You missed a spot," Alessa said suddenly, her voice light and mocking. Elysia glanced up to find her stepsister staring at her, a glass butterfly hovering lazily just above her shoulder. "Or did you want to add it to your collection?"

Elysia's stomach twisted. "I don't—"

"Don't what?" Alessa asked sweetly. The butterfly flitted closer, its wings slicing through the air. "Don't you think glass is beautiful, Elysia? I suppose you wouldn't know. You've never touched it, have you?"

Vivienne smirked, her hands resuming their work as she shaped another rose. "Magic doesn't answer to ashes, sister. She'll never understand it."

Elysia said nothing. Her hands curled tightly around the shard she had picked up, the edges biting faintly into her skin.

They don't know, she reminded herself, swallowing the sharp reply rising in her throat. They don't know what I can do.

"Enough." Lady Seraphine's voice broke through the room like a crack of thunder. "Leave her be, Alessa. If she wastes her time dreaming of things she'll never have, that's no concern of yours."

"Yes, Mother," Alessa said, though the smirk remained on her face as the butterfly dissolved into mist.

Elysia lowered her gaze and continued sweeping, her pulse thrumming like the hum of glass in her veins. She could still feel the weight of the mask she had crafted, hidden safely in her room. It wasn't perfect, no—but it was hers.

It would be enough.

As Alessa and Vivienne resumed their work, their voices rising again in sharp competition, Elysia swept the glass shards into the dustpan, their faint tinkling sound like a promise only she could hear.

They think they own beauty, she thought, her resolve settling like a stone in her chest. They think they own power.

But, they didn't know what she was becoming.

And when she walked into the ball—hidden, perfect, unseen—they wouldn't be able to look away.

The shed was darker tonight. Shadows pooled in the corners like ink, thick and unmoving, as though the very air held its breath. Elysia lit her candle with shaking hands, the flame sputtering weakly before catching, casting long, flickering shapes on the crooked walls.

The mirror was waiting.

Its surface was darker than usual, almost black, as though it had swallowed the light entirely. It seemed to hum faintly, a low vibration just beneath her awareness, so quiet it might have been imagined.

Elysia hesitated, clutching her bandaged hands close to her chest. Her palms still ached from hours of sweeping, but it wasn't just the pain that made her hesitate—it was the memory of Caius's words from last night.

"Glass does not forgive imperfection."

She glanced at the bundle she'd hidden beneath her cloak: the half-finished glass mask, now wrapped in worn cloth. It had been enough to quiet her stepfamily's laughter today. Enough to keep her moving. But, it wasn't perfect.

She knew perfection was the only thing that would let her slip unnoticed into the ball.

Taking a breath, Elysia stepped toward the mirror and pulled the cloth from its surface.

The glass pulsated faintly, shadows skimming across it like dark water. For a moment, nothing happened. Then, the surface stilled, and Caius appeared—his face pale and sharp, his black eyes narrowing the moment he saw her.

"You again," he said, his voice curling through the room like smoke. "You're persistent. I'll give you that."

Elysia straightened, refusing to let him see how her hands trembled. "I need your help again."

Caius arched an eyebrow, his expression a mixture of amusement and disdain. "Help, is it? What could you possibly need now, little cinder-girl? Haven't I already given you enough rope to hang yourself?"

"I'm not here to argue," Elysia replied, ignoring the jab. She reached into her cloak and pulled out the wrapped mask, her fingers lingering on the cloth for a moment before she unwrapped it. The mask caught the faint light of the candle as she held it up.

It was delicate, smooth, and beautiful. But, the crack running through its left side caught the light like a scar.

Caius's gaze fixed on it, his black eyes glittering faintly. "Ah. The mask."

"It's not good enough," Elysia said quietly. "I need to fix it. To finish it. You said the court only respects perfection."

Caius's smile was slow and sharp, more shadow than warmth. "You want me to help you achieve perfection? Foolish girl."

"Is it foolish to want to succeed?" she shot back, surprising herself with the fierceness in her voice.

Caius tilted his head, the shadows behind him twisting as though they could feel her rising resolve. "Success," he murmured. "What does success look like to you, Elysia? A flawless mask? A room full of noble fools staring at you in awe?"

Elysia's grip on the mask tightened. "It looks like freedom. A chance to break my family's curse. A chance to stop being nothing."

The shadows stilled. For a long moment, Caius said nothing, his black eyes unblinking as he studied her. Then, he laughed softly, though the sound held no joy. "You think glass can free you?"

"It's all I have," she said simply.

Caius's expression darkened. "Glass is not a gift, Elysia. It is a cage. You think you control it, but it is already sinking its teeth into you. I see it in your eyes, in your hands."

Elysia frowned, but before she could respond, Caius's

voice dropped lower. "You are walking a path of mirrors, little cinder-girl. Step carefully, or you will bleed."

Elysia looked down at the mask, her breath catching as the crack seemed to gleam faintly in the candlelight. She didn't want to admit it, but Caius's words struck something deep inside her. She could feel it—the glass waiting in her hands, alive and hungry, as though it knew her better than she knew herself.

"Then help me," she said softly, lifting her gaze to meet his. "If the glass is so dangerous, teach me to control it."

Caius's smile vanished, replaced by something colder. "Control?" he asked, his voice soft and dangerous. "Do you think the court respects control? Do you think they will look at you and see anything but a thief playing with fire?"

"I don't care what they see," Elysia replied, the words spilling out before she could stop them. "I won't let them stop me."

Caius leaned closer, his face filling the mirror, his black eyes gleaming like shards of obsidian. "They will stop you, Elysia. The court devours what it does not understand. You will be found. You will be unmade."

The words struck her like a blow, but she held her ground. "I'll make them understand."

Caius stared at her for a long moment, his expression unreadable. Then, slowly, his mouth curled into something that might have been a smile—except there was no warmth in it.

"Very well," he said, his voice soft as silk. "You wish to control the glass? To finish what you've begun?"

"Yes," she whispered.

"Then, you must pay its price."

Elysia's heart skipped. "What price?"

Caius's gaze was steady, unblinking. "Perfection demands sacrifice. The glass will take what you give it, and more. Blood, yes. Will, yes. But, it will also take pieces of you. The mask will hold them, as surely as a mirror holds a reflection."

Elysia shivered. "What happens if I don't finish it?"

"It will finish you," Caius said, his voice dropping to a whisper. "Glass reflects, Elysia. It is beauty, yes—but it is also truth. If your mask cracks before the court, they will see not what you wish to be, but what you are."

His words hung in the air, heavy and sharp as a blade.

Elysia looked down at the mask in her hands, the crack glinting faintly as though mocking her. The candle's light reflected across its surface, casting fractured beams against the walls.

They will see what I am.

"I'll finish it," she said finally, her voice steady.

Caius tilted his head, the shadows flickering faintly behind him like a satisfied sigh. "Then let us hope, little cinder-girl, that you are stronger than you look."

The mirror stilled, Caius's face fading back into the depths of the glass. Elysia stood alone in the cold shed, her hands clutching the mask so tightly the edges bit into her skin.

She looked down at it, her fingers trembling. The hum of glass was quiet now, but she could feel it—waiting, watching.

"I'll finish it," she whispered again, as though speaking the words would make them true.

The candle flickered, its flame guttering briefly before steadying once more.

Outside, the night stretched on, cold and silent, as Elysia turned and slipped back toward the house, the fragile mask held close to her chest.

The dining room was quiet—too quiet. Only the soft clinking of forks against glass plates and the occasional scrape of a chair broke the heavy silence. The room was bathed in the golden glow of candlelight, its warm light gleaming off glassware, polished surfaces, and the sharp edges of silver cutlery.

Elysia moved silently around the table, her apron damp where she'd wiped her hands clean earlier. Lady Seraphine sat at the head of the table, regal and unmoving, her sharp gaze cast down as she sliced precisely through a piece of roasted meat. Across from her, Alessa and Vivienne perched on their chairs like cats—silk gowns draping over the edges, the faint sparkle of glass brooches pinned at their throats.

The glass brooches, of course, were flawless.

Elysia set down a tray of bread, avoiding their eyes as she placed the basket in the center of the table. Her shoulders ached, the burns on her palms hidden beneath fresh wrappings, though every movement tugged at the healing skin.

She used to sit at this very table, back when it was her mother's laughter that filled the room and not the clipped voices of Vivienne and Alessa. Her father had been there too, at the head of the table, his presence steady and warm like the summer sun.

But that was before the sickness swept through the estate, leaving her father bedridden and her mother gone within weeks. Before Lady Seraphine swept in like a winter storm, her lips full of promises that quickly turned to demands.

"Finally," Vivienne muttered as she reached for a roll, her irritation sharp despite the grandeur of the evening. "What took you so long? Did you bake it yourself over the ashes?"

Alessa snorted softly behind her hand. "Careful, Vivienne, or she might start crying again. We wouldn't want tears in the bread."

Elysia said nothing. She tucked the tray under her arm and stepped back, keeping her head low, her hands curling tightly against her sides to steady the tremor in her fingers.

"Enough," Lady Seraphine said coolly, though her tone carried more apathy than reprimand. She didn't even glance up from her plate. "You should focus on your preparations for the ball, instead of snipping at your sister. You can waste your breath later, after the prince has chosen someone else."

Vivienne and Alessa both stiffened, though they masked it poorly. Alessa's lips thinned as she stared at her mother, her eyes flashing with irritation.

"He won't choose someone else," Alessa said, lifting her chin. "Not when he sees what I can do. No one else will bring magic like mine."

Vivienne scoffed. "Butterflies? Everyone knows they're fragile and meaningless." She turned toward Lady

Seraphine. "I'll craft something better, Mother. You'll see. My roses are—"

"Enough," Lady Seraphine said again, sharper this time. "Both of you will create something worthy, or neither of you will go at all."

A tense silence followed, broken only by the slow tap of Lady Seraphine's knife against her plate. The weight of her words hung heavy in the room, settling across their shoulders like a stone.

Elysia moved toward the corner, keeping her steps quiet, but Vivienne's sharp voice stopped her midstride.

"What's wrong with your hands?"

The words struck like a slap. Elysia froze, her back to the table, her pulse quickening as heat climbed up her neck.

Vivienne's chair scraped back, and when Elysia turned, she found her stepsister staring at her with narrowed eyes. "I asked you a question," Vivienne said. "Why are your hands bandaged?"

Elysia glanced quickly at Lady Seraphine, but her stepmother seemed uninterested, her gaze still fixed on her plate. Alessa, however, had leaned forward with sudden interest, her lips curving faintly into a smirk.

"I burned them," Elysia lied, forcing her voice to stay even. "In the kitchen."

Vivienne's gaze didn't waver. Her eyes moved over Elysia's bandaged hands, then flicked up to her face as though searching for cracks in her words. "You've always been clumsy, but that doesn't explain why you've been sneaking around the house like a thief."

Elysia's stomach dropped. "I haven't been—"

"You disappear," Vivienne interrupted, her voice calm but sharp, like the edge of a blade. "At night. I've heard you."

Elysia's throat tightened. "You're imagining things."

"Am I?" Vivienne tilted her head, her dark hair falling across her shoulder as her eyes narrowed further. "It's strange, isn't it? That someone like you—someone so weak and useless—could have anything worth hiding."

Alessa snickered, tearing a roll in half. "Maybe she's been speaking to the mice again. Or whispering her wishes into the ashes."

Vivienne didn't laugh. Her gaze remained fixed on Elysia, cold and calculating, and for one terrible moment, Elysia felt as though Vivienne could see through her— through the mask she wore every day, through the secrets she hid beneath the floorboards and beneath her skin.

"Sit down, Vivienne," Lady Seraphine said at last, her tone laced with irritation. She set her knife down and lifted her gaze to her daughter. "You are wasting time on nonsense."

"But, Mother—"

"Enough," Lady Seraphine snapped. "Focus on yourself, not the girl who sweeps your floors. Do I make myself clear?"

Vivienne clenched her jaw but said nothing as she sank back into her chair, though her glare lingered on Elysia for a moment longer.

Elysia forced herself to move, her steps slow and deliberate as she cleared Alessa's empty plate and carried it to the sideboard. Her mind raced, her pulse thundering in her ears.

Vivienne knows something. Or at least, she suspects.

She had been careful—so careful. But, had she left something behind? A shard of glass, a whisper too loud, a breath too quick? She could feel the weight of the mask in her mind, could hear Caius's voice in her memory. "Glass reflects. Be careful what you show it."

She gripped the plate tighter, feeling the strain in her bandaged hands, the sharp sting of pain grounding her.

They can't know.

The table fell quiet again, though the tension simmered beneath the surface, a crack waiting to spread. Lady Seraphine continued her meal in silence. Vivienne sulked, staring at the flickering candles, while Alessa toyed idly with her glass brooch, her earlier arrogance slowly returning to her face.

And, Elysia stood at the edge of the room, quiet and unseen, the truth of her secrets pressing like glass against her skin.

When the meal ended, she cleared the plates with shaking hands, her body aching with the weight of the day —and the weight of what lay ahead. Vivienne's words clung to her as she climbed the stairs later, echoing in her ears like the hum of glass magic.

"You've been sneaking around... Someone like you could have something worth hiding."

In her room, Elysia leaned against the door, her breath escaping her in ragged bursts. She pressed her forehead to the wood, her heart pounding hard enough to hurt.

Vivienne was watching her now. Watching too closely.

The mask wasn't finished. The gown wasn't ready.

And there were still three days left until the ball.

Three days, Elysia thought, her resolve hardening like iron. Three days to finish what I've started. Three days to be seen.

But as she crossed to the chest at the foot of her bed and pulled the half-finished mask from its hiding place, she noticed the faint crack in its surface had spread—only a little, but enough to make her stomach twist.

Step carefully, Caius had warned her. Glass reflects.

Elysia set the mask down gently on her lap, her fingers brushing over the crack as though to erase it. The hum of magic stirred faintly beneath her skin, low and restless, waiting.

I'll fix it, she thought fiercely, her hands trembling. I have to.

Outside, the wind howled softly through the eaves of the house, its cry low and mournful, like a warning she could not yet understand.

CHAPTER 7

WHISPERS AT COURT

The palace of Solmaris was a place where light lived and shadows lingered. Its walls, spun from glass and stone, rose high enough to pierce the clouds. The crystal spires reflected the midday sun like flames frozen mid-dance, and the great glass dome that crowned the palace turned the light into rivers of gold that spilled across the halls and courtyards.

Inside, the royal court was alive with motion. Artisans bustled through the mirrored corridors, carrying delicate glassworks: chandeliers shaped like blooming roses, birds with wings of crystal, fountains designed to hold sunlight as though it were water. The walls echoed with the sound of tools shaping molten glass into visions of perfection, punctuated by voices—eager, reverent, ambitious.

And, in the center of it all, stood Prince Rilian.

He lingered at the edge of the Great Hall, where preparations for the ball were in full swing. Tall banners were hung from the vaulted ceilings—each one embroidered with symbols of the kingdom, their edges lined with thin glass thread that caught the light like a thousand tiny stars. At the far end of the hall, a group of noble artisans demonstrated their magic, conjuring shapes of glass midair: lions roaring, peacocks spreading their tails, roses opening petal by petal.

But, Rilian wasn't watching the displays.

His eyes, dark as polished onyx, drifted instead across the crowds of courtiers and artisans. His posture was straight, regal, every inch the crown prince his kingdom expected him to be. Yet, there was something about him—something still and distant—that set him apart from the motion swirling around him.

The prince looked tired.

Not outwardly, of course. His face was handsome, his sharp jawline clean-shaven, his dark hair combed into neat waves. He wore a coat of black velvet embroidered with silver thread, and his boots shone like polished glass. But, his eyes were careful—too careful—as though they were searching for something no one else could see.

"Your Highness?"

Rilian turned. A man stood beside him—a royal steward, dressed in crisp black and white, holding a long scroll rolled tightly in his hand. He bowed low, his voice clipped and formal.

"The artisans await your approval, my lord," the steward said. "They wish to display their works before the council arrives."

Rilian's mouth twitched faintly, though it was not quite a smile. "They wish to impress the council, you mean."

"Yes, Your Highness."

The prince looked back at the gathered artisans, his

gaze lingering on the spinning glass animals and roses that hovered midair. They were perfect—flawless, shimmering creations of light and beauty. And yet, to him, they all looked the same.

"What a curious thing it is," Rilian murmured, half to himself, "to watch something so beautiful and feel nothing at all."

The steward hesitated. "My lord?"

"Nothing," Rilian said quickly, his voice turning crisp again. "Send them forward. Let the council see their brilliance."

The steward bowed again and hurried off, leaving the prince alone at the edge of the hall.

Rilian turned away, his eyes drifting upward to the great glass dome overhead. The sunlight poured through it in golden streams, but when Rilian looked closer, he could see faint cracks running through the glass—a spiderweb of fractures so fine they were nearly invisible.

Most people wouldn't notice them.

But, Rilian did.

He had noticed them for weeks now, faint cracks spreading through the oldest glassworks in the palace. The artisans said it was nothing—age, time, imperfections no one could control. But, Rilian had always distrusted convenient answers.

The glass was the pride of Solmaris, the foundation of its power. It couldn't fail. It wouldn't fail.

And yet, as he watched the sunlight filtering through those faint cracks, he couldn't shake the feeling that something was wrong.

"Your Highness!"

The voice shattered his thoughts. Rilian turned to see Lord Alric approaching—a stout man with a booming voice and a cloak lined with crimson glass thread. His broad face was flushed from the effort of weaving through the crowd.

"Prince Rilian," Alric said, bowing so low that his glass medallion clinked against the marble floor. "The council awaits your presence."

"I will join them shortly," Rilian replied, though he made no move to follow.

Lord Alric straightened, eyeing the prince carefully. "The kingdom looks to you, my lord," he said, his voice dropping into a more measured tone. "The ball will be a triumph. The nobility will display their greatest magics, and you will choose the woman most worthy to stand beside you."

"Worthy," Rilian echoed softly, tasting the word like a sour fruit.

"Yes," Alric said, smiling broadly. "It is what the kingdom expects. And what your father demands."

The weight of the words pressed down on Rilian like a hand on his shoulder. He turned his gaze back to the hall, where nobles fluttered about like bright-colored birds, each one draped in glass finery that shimmered in the light. They were all the same—so eager to outshine one another, so eager to prove themselves.

And all of them were hollow.

"I will do what is required," Rilian said finally. His voice was calm, but there was an edge to it, sharp and cold.

"Good," Alric said, clearly satisfied. "Then all will be well."

Rilian said nothing as the councilman swept away, his crimson-lined cloak trailing behind him. The Great Hall was alive with magic and laughter, but Rilian could no longer hear it.

He stared at the spinning glass animals and roses, at the way they sparkled and gleamed, so beautiful and perfect.

But beneath their beauty, he knew, lay fractures.

Elysia could see her breath in the dim light of the candle she carried, the flame flickering wildly as though trying to escape the growing chill. She moved quickly, her shoes barely making a sound against the frost-bitten earth as she slipped inside the cold garden shed and shut the door behind her.

The mirror sat where she had left it, its surface dark and still. For a moment, Elysia hesitated, her fingers trembling faintly where they curled around the candle holder. She could feel the weight of her exhaustion—the bruises beneath her eyes, the burns and cuts hidden beneath bandages, the ache that never quite left her bones anymore. But, it wasn't just her body that felt worn thin. It was something deeper.

"Glass demands sacrifice," Caius had said.

Elysia set the candle down and stepped toward the mirror. Slowly, she pulled the cloth from its surface, the fabric dragging like a sigh as it fell to the floor.

The mirror's surface skimmed outward like water disturbed. Then Caius appeared.

His face emerged from the darkness, pale and sharp as ever, though the edges of his reflection seemed less defined—frayed at the seams, as though the magic that held him there was beginning to unravel. His black eyes fixed on Elysia immediately, narrowing with something between curiosity and disdain.

"You look worse for wear," he said, his voice curling through the room like smoke. "Have the mice been keeping you awake again?"

Elysia ignored the jibe, though her jaw tightened faintly. "It's finished."

Caius arched an eyebrow. "Is it?"

Without a word, Elysia reached into her cloak and drew out the glass mask. She held it up carefully, the candlelight catching its surface and scattering fractured beams across the walls. The mask was beautiful—smooth, gleaming, its shape as delicate and sharp as frost. But, the crack that ran through its left side remained, faint but undeniable, a scar across its perfection.

Caius's gaze lingered on the mask, his expression unreadable. "Interesting," he murmured. "It hums louder than before."

Elysia frowned. "Hums?"

"Do you not hear it?" Caius tilted his head slightly, his dark eyes glinting faintly. "The glass sings, little cinder-girl. It always has. But you..." His gaze drifted to her hands, still wrapped in fresh bandages. "You've given it your blood, haven't you? Your will. A little piece of your-self, tucked away behind its fragile edges."

Elysia swallowed hard, her grip on the mask tighten-ing. She had heard something when she shaped it—something low and distant, like the faint hum of a song she couldn't quite recognize. She hadn't thought much of it at the time, but now…

"What does it mean?" she asked softly.

Caius's expression darkened, shadows curling faintly at the edges of the glass. "It means the mask is no longer just glass. It's yours. It holds your intention, your desire—your reflection. That is what makes it powerful. And dangerous."

Elysia frowned. "But it's not perfect."

"And neither are you," Caius replied sharply. "You think perfection is the key to hiding yourself at the ball? No. Perfection is a lie, Elysia. The court pretends to love it, but what they truly love is power. What you have now— what you hold in your hands—is power."

He leaned closer, his voice dropping lower, darker. "But, power demands its price. That mask will shield you, yes—but it will also betray you if you are not careful. You must hold yourself steady, or the cracks will spread."

Elysia stared at the mask, her pulse quickening as the crack seemed to gleam faintly in the candlelight, like a vein of silver. "How do I stop it?"

"You don't," Caius said softly. "You can't erase what is already broken. But, you can seal it."

Elysia looked up sharply. "How?"

For a moment, Caius said nothing. The shadows behind him shifted restlessly, as though the mirror itself were breathing, and his reflection flickered faintly before steadying again. When he spoke, his voice was quieter— almost reluctant.

"There is a spell," he said. "A final command to bind

the mask to you. It will hold the cracks in place, but the cost will be greater."

"What cost?" Elysia whispered.

Caius's gaze bore into hers, dark and unblinking. "Your strength. Your will. You will feel it pulling at you like a thread, unraveling something deep within. The mask will hold for as long as you do. But if you falter…"

He didn't finish the sentence. He didn't need to.

Elysia's stomach turned, her fingers trembling slightly as she held the mask closer to her chest. "If I don't bind it?"

"Then, it will shatter," Caius replied, his voice as cold as the air around her. "And when it does, they will see you for what you are. The girl who does not belong. The girl who stole magic that was never hers."

Elysia swallowed hard, her throat tight. She looked down at the mask, the faint hum of its magic stirring in her chest like a heartbeat.

"I don't have a choice," she murmured. "If I want to go to the ball—if I want to change anything—I have to finish this."

Caius's smile was slow and sharp, though it held no humor. "Then, you are braver than most."

"Or more desperate," Elysia muttered.

Caius tilted his head, his gaze lingering on her face as though he were seeing something she couldn't. "Perhaps both." He leaned back slightly, the shadows at the edges of the mirror twisting like smoke. "Listen carefully, little cinder-girl. This is what you must do…"

Elysia's hands trembled as Caius explained the final spell—words she would have to whisper into the mask while pouring the last of her will into it. The magic would be raw, demanding, and unforgiving.

But it will hold, she thought, her resolve solidifying like iron beneath her skin. It has to.

When Caius finished speaking, his face seemed fainter in the glass, as though the mirror itself were growing tired. "Remember my warning," he said softly. "You are walking a path of mirrors. Step carefully, or you will bleed."

The shadows fluctuated one last time, and then his reflection vanished, leaving only her own face staring back at her—pale, wide-eyed, and fractured by the cracks in the glass.

Elysia picked up the candle, her grip on the mask tight as she turned toward the door. Outside, the wind howled faintly through the trees, a low, mournful sound that carried through the night like a warning.

She ignored it.

I will finish this, she thought fiercely, her steps quickening as she made her way back toward the house. The spell hummed in her mind, sharp and heavy as a blade.

Three days until the ball.

And the mask had to hold.

The market square buzzed with life, an ocean of bodies pressing close as townsfolk jostled for a better view. Banners of crimson and gold draped from every window, their silk edges shimmering where threads of glass had been woven into their designs. Sunlight caught on the countless decorations hanging across the square—glass stars, roses, and garlands that tinkled faintly in the breeze, as though the air itself hummed with excitement.

Elysia clutched her basket tightly, her shoulders hunched as she stood near the edge of the crowd, beneath the shadow of an awning. She'd accompanied Alessa and Vivienne to the market under Lady Seraphine's orders—something about fresh laces for the ballgowns and dye for their slippers—but her stepsisters had vanished into a shop as soon as they arrived, leaving her to wait.

Now, the crowd surged around her like a living thing, everyone craning their necks to catch a glimpse of the royal procession. Whispers filled the air:

"Have you heard? The prince himself is leading the march!"

"They say he'll choose his bride at the ball."

"Can you imagine? The crown princess!"

Elysia exhaled, her breath catching faintly as she tightened her grip on the basket. Her heart hammered in her chest, though she couldn't quite say why. It's only a parade, she told herself. Only the prince.

But, the words did nothing to steady her.

The hum of glass magic tickled faintly beneath her skin, restless and low. She looked up toward the square where merchants had decorated their stalls with woven glass flowers and tiny figurines that shimmered in the sunlight. Everything here seemed brighter, more alive—as though the very kingdom itself were holding its breath in anticipation.

Then, the crowd fell silent.

Elysia felt it first—a shift in the air, a collective stillness that spread like ripples on water.

A moment later, the royal guards appeared, their polished boots striking the cobblestones in perfect unison. They wore cloaks lined with glass thread that glinted like fire, their armor gleaming with sharp edges of crystal that caught the light. Behind them came musicians, the sound of horns ringing clear and sharp over the square, filling the air with something triumphant.

And then, finally, he appeared.

Prince Rilian.

He rode at the center of the procession atop a black stallion, its mane braided with thin cords of glass that flashed like liquid silver. He wore no crown—only a coat of deep black velvet, lined with silver trim, and a silver pin shaped like a star at his throat. His presence was quiet, powerful, and wholly commanding.

The crowd erupted into cheers, the noise rising like a wave as the prince passed.

Elysia's breath caught.

She had heard the stories, of course. Every girl in the kingdom knew the tales of the handsome prince—his dark hair and sharp eyes, his strength on the battlefield, his quiet charm at court. But, the man before her was not the golden figure whispered of in the streets. He was something else—something heavier.

His face was carved from calm, his gaze sweeping over the crowd with quiet intensity, as though he were searching for something unseen. Up close, there was a weariness to him—a faint shadow beneath his eyes, a tightness in the set of his jaw. He looked less like a prince on a throne and more like a man burdened with an unseen weight.

Why does he look so alone? the thought whispered, unbidden.

Elysia shrank back against the awning as the crowd pressed forward, desperate for a closer look. She kept her eyes on the prince, afraid to blink, as though the image of him might vanish the moment she looked away.

And then, for the briefest of moments, his gaze turned her way.

It happened so quickly that Elysia might have missed it. But she didn't.

Prince Rilian's dark eyes swept over the crowd, sharp and careful, and when they landed on her—just for an instant—they lingered. The space between them seemed to shrink, the noise of the square falling away into nothing.

Elysia's breath froze. She couldn't move. Couldn't think.

Did he see her? Could he see her?

His gaze held no curiosity, no recognition—only a faint flicker of something she couldn't name. Then, his eyes moved on, gliding across the rest of the crowd as though the moment had never happened.

The air returned to her lungs in a rush, and Elysia sagged back against the wall, her heart pounding painfully in her chest. She felt like she'd been struck—not by fear, but by something sharper.

Around her, the crowd continued to cheer, oblivious to the exchange.

"Did you see him?" a woman nearby whispered, her voice full of awe. "He's even more handsome than they say."

"He looked at me," someone else exclaimed.

Elysia turned away, clutching the basket so tightly her knuckles turned white. Her pulse still thundered in her ears, her thoughts tangled and frayed. It doesn't matter, she told herself fiercely. He's just a prince.

But, she knew that wasn't true.

The man on the black stallion wasn't just a prince. He was the key—the bridge between the life she had and the life she wanted. He was a chance to change everything, to lift her family's curse and reclaim what had been stolen.

And, she had three days to prepare for him.

The mask in her room felt heavier than ever, its cracked edges lingering in her thoughts like a whispered warning.

Glass reflects, Caius's voice murmured in her mind. Be careful what you show it.

She pushed the thought away. There was no room for doubt. Not now.

As the last of the procession disappeared down the street, the crowd dispersed, their excitement spilling out in laughter and chatter. Elysia stepped back into the alley, her mind still fixed on the prince, on the way his gaze had lingered—for just a moment.

Perhaps it had meant nothing.

Or perhaps it had meant everything.

Either way, Elysia knew one thing for certain. She would go to the ball. She would finish the mask.

And when she stepped into the palace—hidden, perfect, unseen—she would not be ignored.

CHAPTER 8

THREADS OF FRACTURE

The grand drawing room gleamed with glasswork. Beams of sunlight spilled through the tall windows, catching on polished mirrors and chandeliers until it felt as though the very air was shimmering. The room was alive with motion and tension, the kind that ripples just before something breaks.

Elysia moved carefully across the floor, balancing a tray of tea and honey biscuits. Every step was deliberate, her shoulders drawn in tight to make herself smaller. She was invisible here—just as they liked her to be.

Near the fireplace, Vivienne stood over a long table scattered with rose petals made of glass. Her dark brows knitted together as she cupped molten glass in her hands, reshaping it into another rose. The magic hummed faintly, the soft glow of silver spreading between her fingers as the petals began to form.

"Sharper," Lady Seraphine's voice rang across the room. She sat straight-backed in her chair, her emerald gown pooling elegantly at her feet. Her gaze was cold and unrelenting as it lingered on Vivienne's work. "Your roses need precision, Vivienne. Sharp edges. Let them bleed beauty."

Vivienne gritted her teeth, sweat glistening on her brow as the rose sharpened itself in her hands. A flicker of glass magic danced along the edges of the petals, and when she was done, the rose sat gleaming—a flawless creation of sharp lines and symmetry. It looked so perfect Elysia almost forgot how dangerous it must be to touch.

Vivienne set it down carefully, her face pale but triumphant. "Is this good enough, Mother?"

Lady Seraphine studied it for a long moment before nodding. "Better. But do not let yourself waver. Weakness ruins perfection."

From the chaise near the windows, Alessa's soft laugh drifted across the room. "If roses are all you can do, sister, you might as well not go to the ball at all."

Vivienne shot her a glare. "Say that again, Alessa, and I'll make you a bouquet with thorns."

Alessa ignored her, too engrossed in her own magic. She held one hand aloft, palm upward, and a glass butterfly emerged midair, fluttering to life with an impossibly delicate hum. It was beautiful—so thin it seemed transparent, its wings catching the light and scattering rainbows across the walls.

"See?" Alessa said, smiling faintly as she directed the butterfly to hover above her. "Beauty without trying so hard. The prince will notice me the moment I walk into the room. What will he see you carrying? Roses? How quaint."

Vivienne's jaw tightened, her hands clenching into fists. "At least my magic doesn't break when you touch it."

"I'd rather be delicate than dangerous," Alessa shot back, directing the butterfly to land softly on her outstretched finger.

Elysia placed the tray on the side table, her eyes lingering for a moment on Alessa's butterflies and Vivienne's roses. She said nothing, but her pulse quickened. Both creations were breathtaking, but she could see it—the cracks beneath the surface, the way their rivalry chipped at the edges of their control.

"Do not waste my time with bickering," Lady Seraphine said sharply, silencing them both. "You have tonight and tonight only to perfect your work. The ball is in two days. If either of you falters, you will humiliate this family."

"Yes, Mother," Alessa and Vivienne muttered in unison, though their glares toward each other lingered.

Lady Seraphine turned her gaze on Elysia then, her lip curling faintly as though the sight of her was an irritation she had no patience for. "Elysia, stop hovering like a shadow. Make yourself useful and sweep up the shards."

Elysia glanced at the floor, where fragments of discarded glass roses and butterflies lay scattered like glittering dust. She retrieved the broom and dustpan from the corner of the room, her head down, hands steady.

The shards were sharper than they looked. Even through the thin material of her gloves, she could feel the edges biting against her fingers as she swept them into the dustpan.

"You're too slow," Vivienne snapped, her voice cutting

through the tense silence. "Honestly, how can someone be clumsy and useless at the same time?"

Elysia bit the inside of her cheek to keep from replying.

"Maybe she's distracted," Alessa said, lounging on the chaise with a smile that didn't reach her eyes. "What have you been doing at night, Elysia? You vanish like a ghost. Have you taken up wishing on stars, or is it mice you talk to?"

The words sent a jolt through her, but she kept her head down. Don't react, she told herself. Don't let them see.

Vivienne's gaze sharpened. "That's true, isn't it? You do disappear. And look at your hands." She gestured toward Elysia's bandaged fingers, her voice turning sly. "Still burning yourself on the stove, or are you hiding something?"

Elysia's pulse thundered in her ears. "It's nothing."

"Nothing?" Vivienne said, her voice mocking. "What is it, then? You've been sneaking around like a thief. Maybe you're hiding something worth knowing."

"Vivienne," Lady Seraphine said, her tone carrying the faintest edge of warning. "Leave her. If she wastes her time, let it be her own shame."

Vivienne's lips curled, but she said nothing more. Alessa smirked from her perch on the chaise, her fingers still directing butterflies to spin lazy circles midair.

Elysia forced her hands to stay steady as she dumped the shards into a waste bin. But, she could feel Vivienne's eyes still on her, sharp and searching, as though trying to see through the quiet mask Elysia wore.

Be careful, she reminded herself. You're almost there.

The clock on the mantel chimed softly, the sound filling the heavy silence. Elysia risked a glance at Lady Seraphine, who had closed her eyes as though trying to imagine the ball already won. Alessa and Vivienne returned to their magic, though Vivienne's gaze lingered just a little too long before she looked away.

Elysia's hands curled around the broom handle. Her stepsisters' magic swirled around the room—delicate and deadly, sharp and perfect—but it didn't matter. Soon, their beauty wouldn't matter. Their perfection wouldn't matter.

Because in two days, she would go to the ball.

And when she stepped into the palace—hidden, unseen, flawless—they wouldn't be able to look away.

The garden shed's walls groaned faintly in the cold night wind. A single candle burned on the workbench, its light feeble against the heavy dark that pooled in the corners like ink. Outside, the world was silent—no voices, no footsteps, only the whisper of wind through brittle branches.

Elysia set the glass mask down in the center of the workbench. It gleamed faintly, the crack running through its surface barely visible in the candlelight. Her bandaged hands shook as she unwrapped the thin cloth she had brought, Caius's final words still echoing in her mind.

"Glass demands sacrifice."

The weight of those words sat heavy on her chest as she stared at the mask. It was hers—crafted by her hands, pulled from her will. But, it wasn't finished. Not yet.

She inhaled deeply, forcing her breath to steady as she

traced her fingers over the cold, smooth edges of the glass. It felt alive beneath her touch, thrumming faintly with the hum she'd come to know so well.

"It's just a spell," she whispered, as if saying it aloud would make it easier. "Just one more step."

But, she knew it wasn't that simple.

The shed seemed to know it, too. The air felt heavier here, as though it pressed against her, waiting—watching. The shadows near the mirror flickered faintly, though Caius did not appear. It was better this way. He had told her what to do. Now, it was up to her.

Elysia closed her eyes, whispering the spell under her breath. The words curled from her lips like smoke, strange and sharp, as though they weren't meant for mortal tongues. She opened her eyes and placed her hands on either side of the mask, the candlelight catching on its glass surface and refracting into fractured beams.

The hum grew louder, faint at first, like the stirring of a distant song. Then, it swelled, the sound vibrating through her fingertips, up her arms, and deep into her chest, until it felt as though the glass itself were whispering back to her.

The mask's surface shivered.

Elysia held her breath, her heart pounding, as the crack running through the glass pulsed faintly with silver light.

"It will hold," she told herself, repeating Caius's promise like a prayer. "As long as you do."

She pressed her palms harder against the mask, feeling the cold bite of its edges. The hum rose into a low, keening note, sharp and insistent, like a scream just beyond hearing.

The light grew brighter.

Pain shot through her palms, sharp and sudden. Elysia gasped but didn't pull away. The mask demanded more—she could feel it. It was pulling at her, tugging something vital from deep inside, unraveling her strength thread by thread.

"Take it," she whispered, tears stinging her eyes. "Take what you need."

The hum became a roar, filling the room like a storm, the candle's flame sputtering wildly as though it, too, were afraid. The mask's crack sealed itself slowly, silver light fusing the edges together like molten threads. The surface smoothed, perfect and whole, until the flaw was nothing but a memory.

Elysia's vision blurred. Her arms shook violently, her legs trembling as though they might give way. The mask's pull was relentless, stripping her of something she couldn't name but felt deep in her bones. Her breath came in ragged gasps, and for one terrible moment, she thought she might shatter right alongside the glass.

Then, as quickly as it began, the hum stopped.

The shed fell silent.

Elysia staggered backward, the mask slipping from her fingers. She caught herself against the workbench, her chest heaving, sweat dripping cold down the back of her neck.

The mask lay still on the table, perfectly smooth, its glass surface shining like frozen moonlight.

It was finished.

She stared at it, her vision swimming, her limbs weak and unsteady. The room tilted around her, the edges of her sight darkening like shadows closing in. She felt... less. As though the mask had taken something from her, some piece of herself, and locked it away inside its flawless surface.

Caius's voice echoed faintly in her mind. "The mask will hold for as long as you do."

Elysia reached out with trembling fingers, brushing the glass once more. It was cold—colder than before, like a thing made of ice and magic and secrets. And yet, when her hand touched it, a faint pulse throbbed through her fingers, as though the mask itself were alive.

It's mine, she thought, her heart slowing, steadying. It's ready.

She picked it up carefully, holding it in both hands. The mask's surface reflected the candlelight, fractured and perfect, and for the first time in years, Elysia saw something new in the reflection it cast.

Not a servant. Not a shadow.

Someone seen.

Someone who belonged.

She exhaled shakily and set the mask back down, wrapping it gently in the cloth. Her hands still shook as she tied the knot, the bandages at her wrists faintly stained with new blood.

The shed was silent again, but the magic lingered, watching her.

Elysia turned toward the door, cradling the mask close to her chest. The spell was done. The mask was whole.

And tomorrow, she would wear it.

She stepped out into the night, the cold wind biting at her skin as she made her way back toward the house. The mask's weight seemed to seep into her bones, anchoring her as she walked.

Behind her, the shed sat quiet and dark, but the faint hum of glass lingered in the air like a secret.

Elysia's breath misted faintly as she climbed the narrow wooden stairs, the glass mask wrapped tightly in cloth and cradled against her chest. The weight of it felt heavier tonight, as though the spell that had sealed its cracks was still pulling at her, lingering deep in her bones.

Dust lingered in the cold attic air like old whispers, caught in the slants of moonlight filtering through cracks in the roof. The room smelled of forgotten things-faded lines, rusted locks, broken mirrors tucked away in shadow.

She moved carefully, her slippered feet quiet on the creaking floorboards. In the far corner of the attic, beneath a broken frame draped with an old sheet, sat a battered trunk. It had belonged to her mother—she knew this because Lady Seraphine had banished it here long ago, a remnant of a woman the house no longer spoke of.

The trunk's brass hinges groaned softly as she opened it, the stale air wafting up around her. Inside, lay layers of fabric and memories: a faded cloak, a pair of gloves yellowed with age, a cracked hand mirror lined with tarnished silver. It was as though her mother's life had been packed away in pieces, left to gather dust.

She would understand, Elysia thought, as she carefully

placed the wrapped mask inside. She would see what I'm trying to do.

She began to close the lid—

The creak of a floorboard froze her in place.

Elysia's head shot up, her pulse pounding hard enough to choke her. For a moment, she thought she had imagined it. The attic was always full of strange sounds— wind through the eaves, the house groaning against the night.

But then, she heard it again. A faint shift of weight. A breath.

"Elysia."

The voice cut through the silence like a blade.

Elysia turned sharply, the trunk's lid slamming shut as she rose to her feet. Vivienne stood at the top of the stairs, silhouetted against the faint light from the hallway below. She wore her nightgown, a shawl wrapped around her shoulders, her dark hair loose and disheveled as though she'd come in a hurry.

Her eyes were sharp, gleaming like shards of glass.

"What are you doing up here?" Vivienne demanded, her voice low but dangerous.

Elysia swallowed hard, her heart a wild thing trapped in her chest. "Nothing. I—"

Vivienne stepped into the attic, her gaze sweeping the room. "Nothing?" she said softly, her tone dripping with suspicion. "You've been sneaking off at night. I've heard you. I've seen you. And now, you're here, hiding... something."

"I'm not hiding anything," Elysia said quickly, though her voice sounded thin even to her own ears.

Vivienne's gaze dropped to the trunk, where Elysia stood as though guarding it. "What's in there?"

"Nothing."

"Move."

"No."

The word slipped out before Elysia could stop it, and Vivienne's head snapped up sharply, her lips curling into a smile that held no warmth.

"Excuse me?"

Elysia's hands curled into fists at her sides, though they trembled faintly. "It's none of your business. Go back to bed, Vivienne."

Vivienne laughed softly, a sound like shattered glass. "None of my business? You think I haven't noticed you skulking around like a rat? Your bandaged hands, the way you disappear without a word? You're up to something, aren't you?" She stepped closer, her eyes narrowing. "Are you stealing from us? Plotting something? You've always been jealous of us—jealous of me."

"I don't know what you're talking about."

"Don't lie to me!" Vivienne's voice rose, sharp and accusing, echoing faintly through the attic. She stepped closer, her bare feet whispering across the floorboards as though she were stalking prey. "What are you hiding, Elysia?"

"Nothing."

Vivienne's gaze burned into her, relentless. "Let me see." She moved toward the trunk, her fingers outstretched.

Elysia stepped in front of it, her body blocking Vivienne's path. "I said no."

Vivienne froze. For a moment, the silence was deafening. Then, her expression shifted—her smile sharpening into something cruel and triumphant. "You are hiding something."

"I'm not."

"Then, why won't you let me see?"

Elysia said nothing, her breath coming in short, shallow bursts. The attic suddenly felt smaller, darker, the shadows pressing in on all sides.

Vivienne tilted her head, her voice dropping to a mocking whisper. "What could someone like you possibly have worth hiding? Did you steal it? Or did you dream it up, the way you always do?" She leaned closer, her eyes glinting. "You don't belong anywhere, Elysia. You're nothing—less than nothing. A shadow pretending to be more."

Elysia's vision blurred, her fists trembling at her sides as the words struck like a blade. But, she didn't move.

Vivienne reached for the trunk again. "Move aside—"

"I said no!"

The words burst from Elysia's lips like a crack of thunder. The air convulsed around her, a sudden pulse that rattled through the floorboards and sent a whisper of sound skimming through the room.

Vivienne stumbled back, her hand jerking away as though she'd been burned. "What was that?"

Elysia froze.

Vivienne stared at her, her face pale in the moonlight, her eyes wide with something like fear. "What did you do?" she whispered.

Elysia's pulse roared in her ears. She could feel the

faint hum of glass magic curling beneath her skin, responding to her anger—her fear. The mask was quiet, hidden safely in the trunk, but its presence lingered in the air like a held breath.

Vivienne took another step back, her gaze flicking toward the trunk, then back to Elysia. "There's something wrong with you," she said, her voice low and uncertain. "You're hiding something. I know it."

"Leave," Elysia said quietly, her voice steadier than she felt.

Vivienne hesitated for a long moment, her eyes narrowing. Then, she turned sharply on her heel, her shawl whipping behind her as she stormed back toward the stairs.

"This isn't over," she snapped over her shoulder. "I'll find out what you're hiding. And when I do, you'll regret it."

The stairs creaked as she descended, her footsteps sharp and angry, until the sound faded into silence.

Elysia sagged against the trunk, her knees giving way as she sank to the floor. Her breath came in ragged gasps, her heart hammering so hard it hurt.

That was close.

The hum of the magic had faded, but she could still feel it—like a flicker of warmth lingering deep beneath her skin. She pressed a hand to her chest, trying to steady her breathing.

Vivienne knew something was wrong. She could feel it.

Two days, Elysia thought, her gaze drifting toward the closed trunk. I just have to hold on for two more days.

She pushed herself upright, her legs unsteady, and

stared at the moonlight spilling across the floorboards. It glowed silver, sharp and beautiful, like the mask hidden beneath the trunk's lid.

Vivienne's words still echoed in her mind, sharp as thorns. You're nothing. A shadow pretending to be more.

But, Elysia clenched her fists, her resolve hardening like iron.

Not for long.

CHAPTER 9

THREADS TIGHTEN

The garden shed loomed in the moonlight, its edges blurred by the thick mist curling across the ground. Elysia slipped inside, clutching the mask tightly in her bandaged hands. The air was damp and cold, heavy with a silence that felt alive, as though the shed itself were holding its breath.

She lit a single candle, the flame trembling against the draft. Its glow barely pushed back the darkness, but it was enough to illuminate the workbench where she set the mask down.

Her heart raced as she unwrapped it, the cloth falling away to reveal smooth glass gleaming like a captured star. The mask was flawless now, the crack sealed by the spell she had poured her strength into. It hummed faintly as she lifted it, the sound too soft to hear but loud enough to feel, like a pulse beneath her fingertips.

Elysia inhaled deeply. It's time.

She raised the mask to her face.

The moment the glass touched her skin, the hum grew louder, filling her ears with a low, resonant tone. It wasn't painful—at least, not yet—but it was relentless, vibrating through her bones and down to her very core.

The world blurred.

Elysia stumbled, gripping the workbench to steady herself as the mask's magic surged around her. The air felt alive, charged with energy that pressed against her from every angle, pulling at her like invisible hands.

Breathe, she told herself. Just breathe.

The hum softened, and when she opened her eyes, the shed was no longer the same. The candle's light was sharper, brighter, casting shadows that danced across the walls, like living things. The air shimmered faintly, and for a moment, Elysia thought she could see tiny fractures in the glass jars and tools scattered across the bench—imperfections that hadn't been there before.

She turned to the mirror.

What she saw made her breath catch.

The reflection staring back at her was... her, but not the her she had always known. The mask had smoothed the lines of exhaustion from her face, softened the angles of her jaw, brightened the dull gray of her eyes until they gleamed like polished silver.

It wasn't a disguise—not exactly. It was as though the mask had taken her and reshaped her into something more. Something brighter, sharper, and almost... unreal.

She reached up to touch her face, and the reflection did the same, her fingers brushing the mask's edges. It felt warm now, as though it had fused with her skin, humming faintly with each beat of her heart.

But, there was something else.

As she stared at her reflection, she noticed faint tendrils of light curling outward from the mask, trailing down her neck and across her shoulders like threads of molten glass. They shimmered faintly, almost invisible, but when she moved, they followed—an extension of the magic, binding her to the mask in ways she couldn't see.

Elysia's breath quickened. The mask wasn't just a tool. It was part of her now.

The hum grew louder again, and with it came a faint pressure at the edges of her mind. It wasn't overwhelming, but it was enough to make her stomach twist. She closed her eyes, willing the sensation away, but it lingered, a constant reminder of the power she had claimed—and the cost she was paying.

When she removed the mask, the world dimmed. Her reflection in the mirror returned to what it had always been: tired, pale, and ordinary.

Elysia's knees buckled, and she caught herself against the workbench, her breath escaping in ragged gasps. Her strength was gone, drained as though the mask had pulled it straight from her veins.

She stared at the mask, now resting on the bench. Its surface was as smooth and beautiful as before, but it seemed to watch her, silent and waiting.

"I'll make it work," she whispered, her voice hoarse. "I'll wear it. I'll hold it together."

The words felt like a promise—a fragile, dangerous promise.

Elysia reached for the cloth and wrapped the mask again, her hands trembling as she tied the knot. Her body felt weaker than before, as though the magic had left a hollow space where her strength should have been.

But, her resolve hadn't faltered.

The mask was ready. She would wear it to the ball.

And when she stepped into the palace, they wouldn't see the girl who swept floors and hid in the shadows.

They would see someone new.

The hallway was dim, lit only by the faint moonlight filtering through the tall windows at the end of the corridor. Elysia crept toward her room, the glass mask wrapped tightly in cloth and cradled against her chest. Her steps were soft, her breath held, as though the house itself might wake and catch her.

The door to her room was just a few feet away. Almost there.

"Elysia."

The voice froze her in place.

She turned slowly, her heart hammering against her ribs, to see Vivienne step out of the shadows. Her stepsister was still dressed in her nightgown, a heavy shawl draped around her shoulders, her dark hair loose and wild as though she'd been pacing her room.

But, it was Vivienne's eyes that struck fear into Elysia's chest—sharp, gleaming, and hungry.

"You've been sneaking around again," Vivienne said, her voice low and dangerous.

Elysia tightened her grip on the bundle in her arms. "Go back to bed, Vivienne."

Vivienne's lips curled into a smile that held no warmth. "Not until you tell me what you're hiding."

"I'm not hiding anything," Elysia said, forcing her voice to stay steady.

"Don't lie to me." Vivienne took a step closer, her bare feet silent against the floor. "You've been skulking around for weeks now, disappearing into the night. And those hands—" She gestured toward Elysia's bandaged fingers. "What have you been doing, Elysia? Playing with fire? Or something worse?"

"It's none of your business," Elysia replied, though her pulse thundered in her ears.

Vivienne laughed softly, the sound sharp and bitter. "None of my business? Do you think I don't see you? Do you think I haven't noticed how you watch us? How you listen to everything we say?" She leaned closer, her voice dropping to a venomous whisper. "You think you're clever, don't you? Hiding in the shadows, pretending to be invisible. But you're not. I see you, Elysia. I always have."

Elysia's grip on the mask tightened, the rough cloth biting into her palms. "If you've always seen me," she said quietly, "then why haven't you ever looked?"

The words hung in the air, sharp as glass.

For a moment, Vivienne faltered, her expression flickering with something unreadable. But, the moment passed, and her smile returned, colder than before.

"You're deflecting," she said. "But, it doesn't matter. I'll find out what you're hiding. And when I do, I'll make sure Mother knows. Do you think she'll let you stay after that?"

Elysia felt her chest tighten, her fear pressing like a weight against her ribs. But beneath the fear, something else stirred—something sharp and unyielding.

"Do you think she'd believe you?" Elysia asked, her voice steady despite the tremor in her hands.

Vivienne's smile faltered again. "What did you say?"

Elysia took a step forward, her gaze locking with Vivienne's. "You don't know anything about me. You think you see me, but you don't. You never have. And, you never will."

The hallway seemed to hold its breath, the tension between them crackling like the hum of distant glass.

Vivienne's eyes narrowed, her lips curling into a sneer. "You're nothing, Elysia. Nothing but ash pretending to be something more."

Elysia's pulse roared in her ears, but she didn't look away. "We'll see," she said softly.

Vivienne stared at her for a long moment, the silence between them heavy and charged. Then, with a sharp twist of her shawl, she turned on her heel and stalked back down the hallway.

"This isn't over," she said over her shoulder. "I'll find out what you're hiding. And when I do, you'll regret it."

Elysia stood still for a long moment, her breath coming in short, sharp bursts. Her hands trembled as she clutched the mask tighter against her chest, the hum of its magic faint but steady beneath the cloth she'd wrapped it in.

Vivienne hadn't seen it—Elysia had made sure of that. She'd kept the mask hidden beneath her shawl, pressing it close to her body to muffle its glow. It was a risk bringing it out of the attic, but leaving it there after Vivienne's intrusion wasn't safe anymore.

Vivienne was a threat now—more than she had been before.

But Elysia's resolve didn't waver.

She turned and slipped into her room, closing the door behind her with trembling fingers. The moonlight streamed through the small window, casting faint beams across the floor.

Crossing to the chest at the foot of her bed, she carefully placed the mask inside, her hands lingering for a moment on the cloth-wrapped bundle. The attic had been her hiding place for so long, but it wasn't an option anymore. Not after last night. If Vivienne had any inkling of what the mask was—or worse, what Elysia planned to do with it—there would be no way to stop her.

Vivienne's words pressed against her mind, but she pushed them aside, focusing instead on what lay ahead.

The ball was tomorrow.

And when she stepped into the palace, no one—Vivienne, Alessa, or Lady Seraphine—would stop her.

CHAPTER 10

INTO THE LIGHT

The room was silent except for the faint sound of the wind rattling the shutters. Elysia sat on the edge of her narrow bed, the chest open before her. Moonlight spilled through the small window, casting pale beams across the glass gown folded carefully inside, its surface catching the light and refracting it into faint, fleeting rainbows.

Her hands trembled as she reached for the mask. It was still wrapped in cloth, the fabric hiding the smooth, cold surface that seemed to hum faintly even now.

This is it, she thought. Her heart thudded in her chest, each beat a drumbeat of anticipation.

Elysia unwrapped the mask first, her fingers brushing over the delicate glass edges. It gleamed faintly in the moonlight, its surface flawless now—untouched by the crack that had once run through it. She'd spent hours repairing it, stitching the broken shards back together with fragile, whisper-thin magic.

She lifted it carefully, the hum of its power growing louder, resonating in her chest like a second heartbeat.

The gown came next. She had made it herself, every stitch woven with tempered spells meant to keep the fragile glass intact. Even now, as she ran her hands over its shimmering layers, she marveled at the way it seemed to flow like water, alive with quiet magic. Yet she could feel its tension beneath her fingertips—a fragility that mirrored the mask.

Still, there was no room for doubt.

With deliberate hands, she slipped the gown over her head. It clung to her like a second skin, the cool fabric settling against her as though it had been waiting for her to move inside it. The shimmering folds caught the moonlight as she turned to the mirror, her reflection staring back at her—pale, tired, and shaking slightly as she reached for the mask.

Elysia turned back to the mask, its hum growing louder as she picked it up. Her breath caught as she raised it to her face, the cold glass brushing her skin.

The hum exploded into sound, filling her ears and vibrating through her bones. For a moment, the world tilted, the edges of her vision blurring as the magic surged around her, through her.

And then, it was quiet.

She opened her eyes.

The reflection staring back at her wasn't quite hers.

Her face was the same, but the mask had reshaped it subtly—softening the angles, sharpening her eyes, giving her features a faint, otherworldly glow. The scars and exhaustion she had worn like armor were gone, replaced by something smooth, flawless, and almost unrecognizable.

She stepped closer to the mirror, her hand reaching up to touch her face. The mask felt warm now, as though it had fused with her, its edges melting into her skin. She turned her head, watching the light play across the glass, her heart pounding as she realized what the mask had done.

She looked... perfect.

But beneath the perfection, she could feel the magic's pull—a steady, faint tug that drained her strength even now. The mask wasn't just an object. It was alive, bound to her in ways she couldn't fully understand.

"Glass demands sacrifice," Caius's voice whispered in her mind.

Elysia pulled away from the mirror, her hands trembling as she turned toward the window. The moon hung high in the sky, its light bright and cold, reminding her of the time slipping away.

She reached for the cloak draped over the back of the chair. It was simple, made of thick wool, its dark fabric a sharp contrast to the shimmering gown beneath. She pulled it around her shoulders, the weight of the fabric grounding her, hiding the glow of the glass.

The mask stayed in place, its hum faint but steady, like a heartbeat just beneath her own.

She turned back to the mirror one last time.

The girl staring back at her looked like someone new.

Not a servant. Not a shadow.

Someone powerful. Someone seen.

Elysia exhaled slowly, her breath fogging the glass. It was time.

She gathered the edges of her cloak, pulling them tight as she stepped toward the door. Her steps were slow, deliberate, the weight of the mask and the gown pressing against her like an invisible hand.

When she reached the door, she paused, her hand hovering over the latch. For a moment, doubt flickered in her chest.

What if it fails? What if they see through me?

She clenched her fists, the bandages beneath her gloves pulling tight against her skin.

No. I will not fail. They will see me.

With a steadying breath, Elysia pushed the door open and stepped into the hallway.

The house was silent, the shadows thick and unmoving. Her footsteps were soft against the wooden floor as she moved toward the stairs, her heart pounding in her ears.

At the door to the garden, she hesitated, her hand resting against the cold brass handle. Beyond it lay the road to the palace, the path to everything she had worked for.

She pulled the door open and stepped outside.

The night was cold, the wind biting at her cheeks as she pulled the cloak tighter around her shoulders. The mask hummed faintly, its warmth a sharp contrast to the chill in the air.

Elysia looked up at the moon, her breath misting in the dark. Then, she turned toward the road and began to walk.

The palace awaited.

The road to the palace stretched ahead, shrouded in mist and shadow. The moon hung low in the sky, its pale light brushing against the frost-covered ground. Elysia's footsteps were soft but steady, her cloak wrapped tightly around her to shield her from the cold.

The mask hummed faintly against her face, the sound pulsing in time with her heartbeat. It was quieter now, as though the magic it carried was resting, conserving its strength. But every so often, the hum would rise, a sharp vibration that sent a shiver down her spine, a reminder of the power she carried—and the cost it demanded.

Her hands tightened on the edges of her cloak as she walked, her breath fogging in the chill night air. The path ahead was empty, silent save for the crunch of her footsteps on the frozen ground.

You're almost there, she told herself.

But, the quiet left too much room for her thoughts.

Doubt whispered at the edges of her mind, weaving its way through the hum of the mask. What if the mask doesn't hold? What if they see through it?

She shook her head sharply, as though the motion could scatter the thoughts like smoke. The mask would hold. It had to.

Still, the weight of the night pressed against her chest, heavy and unrelenting. Her steps slowed as she approached a bend in the road, her gaze drawn to the shimmering surface of a puddle at the edge of the path.

The moonlight reflected off the water, casting a faint glow that rippled gently in the breeze. Elysia hesitated, then crouched beside it, her reflection staring back at her from the glassy surface.

Her breath caught.

The mask had reshaped her, softened her, turned her into someone new. But here, in the rippling water, she thought she could see something else beneath it—a faint shadow of the girl she used to be, flickering like a candle on the edge of going out.

Is this who I am now?

The thought lingered, heavy and cold, but she pushed it aside.

You're not that girl anymore.

She rose to her feet, her fingers brushing against the mask's edges as though to reassure herself it was still there. The hum steadied, and so did her breathing. She pulled her cloak tighter and pressed forward.

The road turned again, and this time, the trees opened to reveal a sight that stole her breath.

The palace rose in the distance, its towers piercing the sky like shards of glass. Light poured from its windows, spilling out into the night and illuminating the frost-covered fields surrounding it. The great glass dome at its center gleamed like a captured star, its surface refracting the moonlight into a thousand glittering fragments.

Elysia stopped in her tracks, her heart pounding.

The sight was beautiful—so beautiful it hurt. It was a world she had dreamed of for so long, a world of light and magic and power. A world she had no place in.

But tonight, she would step into it.

Her hands trembled as she adjusted the edges of her cloak. The palace gates weren't far now, their dark iron frames standing tall against the light spilling from the courtyard beyond. She could see figures moving near the entrance—nobles in shimmering gowns and cloaks, their glass magic swirling faintly around them like living things.

Her pulse quickened.

They'll notice me.

No, she told herself fiercely. They'll notice the mask. The gown. The person you've become.

She took a steadying breath and stepped forward, the crunch of frost beneath her boots grounding her. The road narrowed as it approached the gates, the mist thinning until it was nothing but a faint shimmer at her heels.

As she drew closer, the hum of the mask grew louder, a steady vibration that filled her ears and settled deep in her chest. The weight of it pressed against her, heavy but not unbearable.

It's working.

The guards at the gate didn't spare her a second glance as she passed. She kept her head down, her steps measured, her cloak wrapped tightly around her to hide the gown's glow.

The courtyard was alive with movement and sound— nobles and artisans mingling beneath the glow of glass chandeliers that hovered in midair. The air buzzed with magic, faint whispers of glass creations flitting through the crowd like sparks.

Elysia paused at the edge of the courtyard, her breath catching as she took it all in.

It was everything she had imagined—beauty and power and danger, all wrapped in light and shadow.

But, there was no time to linger.

She moved forward, her cloak brushing against the cobblestones as she approached the towering doors of the palace. A servant opened one of them for her, his expression polite but indifferent, and she stepped inside.

The hum of the mask softened as the warmth of the palace enveloped her, but the weight of what lay ahead pressed heavier than ever.

She straightened her shoulders, her hands tightening on the edges of her cloak.

The ballroom was just ahead.

The sound hit her first—a swell of music and voices, laughter and applause, all blending into a shimmering hum that filled the air. It spilled through the open doors of the ballroom and washed over Elysia as she stepped across the threshold.

Her breath caught in her throat.

The ballroom was unlike anything she had ever imagined.

It was vast, its high ceilings supported by gleaming crystal pillars that seemed to rise forever. Chandeliers hung suspended in midair, their glass facets catching the light and throwing it across the room in a cascade of rainbows. The walls were lined with mirrors that reflected the scene back upon itself, creating the illusion of endless space.

The nobles moved like living art, their gowns and cloaks shimmering with threads of glass magic. Butterflies flitted in delicate arcs above their heads, glass roses bloomed in floating bouquets, and faint trails of frost curled across the marble floor beneath their feet.

For a moment, Elysia stood frozen in the doorway, her cloak still drawn tightly around her shoulders.

This is it.

Her heart pounded as she stepped forward, her boots clicking softly against the polished floor. She kept her head down, her face half-hidden by the hood of her cloak, but she could feel the eyes of the crowd brushing against her like a faint breeze.

No one stopped her.

The mask hummed faintly against her skin, its magic settling over her like a second layer of armor. She straightened her shoulders, her steps growing steadier as she moved deeper into the room.

The air was heavy with magic. Elysia could feel it pressing against her, swirling faintly in the space between the chandeliers and the polished floor. It shimmered in the glass decorations and lingered in the folds of the nobles' gowns.

She glanced toward the far end of the room, where a dais rose above the crowd. At its center stood the royal family's crest, a towering glass sculpture shaped like a crown, its edges sharp and gleaming. The light refracted through it, casting sharp patterns across the walls like a net of stars.

And beneath it stood the prince.

Elysia's breath faltered.

Prince Rilian was a striking figure, his dark hair gleaming faintly in the light of the chandeliers. He wore a deep blue coat lined with silver thread, the crest of

Solmaris pinned at his shoulder. His posture was regal but unassuming, his hands clasped behind his back as he scanned the room with quiet intensity.

Even from a distance, Elysia could sense the weight he carried—an invisible crown resting heavily on his brow.

He didn't move as nobles approached him in pairs and groups, bowing and offering their introductions. He nodded politely but said little, his gaze flicking toward the crowd as though searching for something—or someone.

Elysia's pulse quickened.

She moved toward the edge of the room, slipping between clusters of nobles. Her cloak brushed against the marble floor, the faint glow of her gown hidden beneath its folds.

A servant passed her, offering a tray of sparkling drinks. She shook her head and turned toward the mirrors lining the wall, her reflection catching her attention for just a moment.

The mask.

Even hidden beneath her hood, it transformed her. The faint hum of its magic seemed to flutter across the glass, distorting her reflection until she hardly recognized herself.

She inhaled deeply, her hands tightening on the edges of her cloak.

You're here, she told herself. *No one knows who you are. They can't touch you.*

The hum of the mask softened, steadying her breath.

She turned back toward the center of the room and froze.

The prince was looking at her.

For a fleeting moment, their eyes met across the crowd.

Elysia's heart skipped a beat, her pulse roaring in her ears. She couldn't move, couldn't breathe, caught in the quiet intensity of his gaze.

It wasn't curiosity—not entirely. There was something sharper there, something searching, as though he could sense the faint hum of the glass magic that surrounded her.

But before she could think to react, someone approached the prince—a noblewoman in a gown of shimmering silver—and his gaze shifted.

Elysia exhaled shakily, her hand flying to her chest as though to steady her pounding heart.

He had seen her.

Only for a moment, but it was enough.

Her fingers brushed against the mask, the hum faint but constant beneath her touch. She pulled her cloak tighter and stepped back into the shadows at the edge of the room.

The night was only beginning.

CHAPTER 11

THE DANCE OF
SHADOWS

The ballroom's edge felt safer, its shadows deeper and quieter, a place where Elysia could observe without being seen. She lingered there, her cloak still drawn around her shoulders, watching as the nobles moved like living constellations under the shimmering chandeliers.

Glass magic danced everywhere.

A noblewoman raised her hand, and a dozen butterflies of molten glass exploded into being, their wings refracting the light as they scattered above her. Nearby, a man conjured a pair of crystal foxes that darted between the crowd, their movements so lifelike they almost seemed alive.

Everywhere she looked, there was beauty and brilliance—magic spun into fragile, shimmering forms, each one designed to outshine the next.

Elysia's pulse quickened. This was the world she had stepped into: dazzling and sharp, beautiful and dangerous.

The mask hummed faintly against her skin, a steady

vibration that reminded her of its presence, its power. But beneath the hum, she could feel something else—a faint tension, like a string pulled too tight.

Hold together, she told herself. Just hold together.

She let her gaze drift across the room, her eyes catching on familiar figures near the center of the crowd.

Alessa stood with her head held high, her gown of pale gold catching the light like morning sunlight on glass. A flock of her signature butterflies hovered around her, their wings glowing faintly as they circled in delicate arcs.

Beside her, Vivienne was radiant in crimson, her sharp-edged roses twining around her like a thorny crown. Her dark eyes scanned the room with the precision of a blade.

They were radiant. Perfect.

And utterly unaware of her presence.

Her stepsister didn't pause, didn't look twice, but Elysia's breath still hitched.

They don't know it's you, she reminded herself. They can't see through the mask.

But even as she told herself that, she could feel the mask's weight pressing faintly against her temples.

She turned toward the mirrors lining the walls, letting her gaze flicker to her own reflection.

Her breath caught.

The mask had smoothed her edges, softened her features, turned her into something extraordinary. But in the flickering light of the chandeliers, she thought she could see something else—a faint crack running through her reflection, a distortion that wasn't there before.

Her pulse quickened.

Caius warned you, the thought whispered, sharp and cold. *Glass reflects. Be careful what you show it.*

Elysia clenched her hands into fists beneath her cloak, willing the reflection to steady. When she looked again, it was gone—her face flawless once more, the mask holding strong.

But, the hum lingered, faint and insistent.

She turned away from the mirrors, her gaze drawn back to her stepsisters. Vivienne was leaning toward Alessa now, her lips moving in a sharp whisper. Alessa tilted her head, following Vivienne's gaze toward the edge of the room—toward Elysia.

Her stomach twisted.

Don't panic.

She stepped deeper into the shadows. The faint hum of the mask steadied her breath, but her heart still pounded as she felt their eyes skimming over her.

Vivienne's expression shifted—something between curiosity and suspicion flickering across her face. She said something to Alessa, who nodded, and they turned back toward the crowd, their conversation dissolving into laughter.

Elysia exhaled shakily.

They hadn't recognized her. Not yet.

But, Vivienne had noticed her. She could feel it in the sharpness of her gaze, the tension in the air that seemed to tighten every time their paths came close to crossing.

The mask hummed again, louder this time, and Elysia pressed her hand to her chest, willing it to quiet.

You can't let them see you falter.

She took a deep breath, her hands steadying as she

adjusted the edges of her cloak. The noise of the ballroom swirled around her—music and laughter and the faint crackle of glass magic—but she forced herself to focus, to blend in.

The night was still young.

And this was only the beginning.

The ballroom floor gleamed beneath the chandeliers, a sea of polished marble lit by the cascading glow of glass magic. Elysia stood at the edge of it, her cloak still drawn tightly around her shoulders. She could feel the weight of the crowd pressing against her, their voices weaving together into a low hum that thrummed in her chest.

The mask hummed faintly in response, its vibration steady and insistent.

It's time.

She exhaled slowly, her hands tightening on the edges of her cloak. Then, with a quiet resolve, she stepped forward.

Her first step was careful, almost hesitant, but the next came more easily, her boots clicking softly against the marble. Each step pulled her further from the safety of the shadows and closer to the center of the room, where the light was brightest, the gazes sharpest.

Heads began to turn.

Elysia kept her face angled downward, her hood still concealing the edges of the mask, but she could feel the weight of their eyes on her. Whispers followed in her wake, faint and curious, like the brush of leaves in the wind.

"Who is she?"

"Her gown—it's like nothing I've ever seen."

"Is she wearing a mask?"

The voices blurred together, and Elysia forced herself to keep moving, her steps measured and deliberate. She reached the heart of the ballroom, the chandeliers above casting their fractured light over her, illuminating the faint shimmer of her gown beneath the cloak.

The mask's steady vibration seemed to ripple through her chest. It wasn't painful—not yet—but it was enough to remind her of its presence, its power.

She glanced toward the dais, where Prince Rilian still stood beneath the towering glass crest. He hadn't moved, his hands clasped behind his back as he observed the crowd with quiet intensity. His dark eyes swept across the room, sharp and searching, as though he were looking for something—or someone.

Her breath caught.

The hum of the mask deepened, a faint pull that seemed to draw her closer to him, and she hesitated for the briefest moment.

"Look at her," a sharp voice whispered from somewhere nearby.

Elysia's pulse quickened. She turned her head slightly, her gaze catching on a familiar pair of figures near the edge of the crowd.

Alessa and Vivienne.

They stood close together, their gowns glowing faintly in the light of the chandeliers. Alessa's butterflies fluttered around her in delicate arcs, their wings scattering rainbows across her golden gown. Vivienne's sharp-edged roses twined around her like living flames, their crimson glow casting shadows across her features.

And both of them were staring at her.

Vivienne's gaze was sharp and unblinking, her lips curving into a faint, knowing smile. Alessa leaned close to her sister, whispering something, and Vivienne's expression darkened.

Keep moving.

Elysia forced herself to turn away, her steps quickening as she crossed the floor. The hum of the mask steadied her, its pull anchoring her even as her pulse roared in her ears.

They don't know it's you. They can't.

But, she could feel their eyes burning into her back, sharp and relentless.

As she neared the dais, the whispers around her grew louder.

"Do you see her gown? It's... glowing."

"Her mask is unlike anything I've seen before."

"Do you think she's from Solmaris? Or another kingdom?"

Elysia didn't respond, didn't acknowledge the voices. She kept her head high, her steps measured, her hands steady beneath the folds of her cloak.

The prince turned his head.

Her breath caught again as their eyes met across the remaining distance. His gaze was calm but searching, his dark eyes narrowing faintly as he studied her. It was as though he could sense something in the air, a faint hum of magic that no one else seemed to notice.

Elysia's steps slowed. The mask's vibration wobbled through her like a second heartbeat. Her chest tightened as she felt its pull grow stronger, its weight pressing against her skin.

She was close now, just a few steps away from the base of the dais. The prince's gaze didn't waver, and for a moment, she felt as though the rest of the room had fallen away, leaving only the two of them.

The mask's hum became a roar.

She faltered, the edges of her vision blurring faintly as the strain of the magic pressed against her. She willed herself to hold steady.

Not yet. Just a little longer.

She forced herself to take another step, her gaze locking with his. The prince tilted his head slightly, his expression unreadable, and Elysia felt a flicker of unease curl in her chest.

He wasn't just looking at her.

He was seeing her.

Her pulse thundered in her ears as she reached the base of the dais, her legs trembling faintly beneath the weight of the mask. The hum quieted, but its presence lingered, heavy and insistent.

The prince opened his mouth as though to speak, but before he could, a servant approached him, bowing low and murmuring something Elysia couldn't hear.

The moment broke.

Elysia stepped back, her hands tightening on the edges of her cloak as she slipped into the crowd. Her breath came in short, shallow bursts, her chest aching from the strain of the mask.

She could still feel his gaze on her, even as she turned away.

Elysia hovered at the edge of the dais, her hands clenched tightly beneath her cloak. The mask hummed faintly now, the vibration pulsing through her like a warning, though the crowd around her seemed oblivious.

She had felt his gaze on her long before she turned back toward him.

Prince Rilian stood at the center of the dais, his posture regal but unassuming, his hands resting lightly behind his back. He watched her again, his dark eyes fixed on her with an intensity that seemed to cut through the noise and light of the ballroom.

Elysia's breath caught as their eyes met once more.

The mask hummed louder, the pull of its magic sharp against her skin. She straightened her shoulders, forcing her hands to relax as she took a tentative step forward.

The movement caught his attention.

The prince tilted his head slightly, his expression calm but curious. There was no hostility in his gaze, but it unsettled her all the same—like a sharp knife pressed against glass, testing for cracks.

"Your Highness," a courtier murmured, bowing low as he approached the prince. But Rilian raised a hand, a subtle gesture that dismissed him without a word.

His focus didn't waver.

Elysia swallowed hard. The mask hummed again, the vibration growing deeper, and she could feel the weight of it pressing against her temples, her chest. It wasn't just the magic—it was him. The way he looked at her, as though he could see beyond the shimmering gown and the flawless mask, beyond the illusion she had so carefully crafted.

The crowd around her seemed to fall away, the noise fading into a distant hum.

"You're not dancing," Rilian said finally, his voice cutting through the silence like a blade.

Elysia blinked, startled. His voice was lower than she expected, steady and calm, but laced with something sharper.

She opened her mouth to respond, but her throat felt dry, her thoughts tangled. The mask hummed louder, its pull more insistent, and she steadied herself.

"I... prefer to observe," she said finally, her voice quiet but steady.

The prince raised an eyebrow, his lips curving into the faintest hint of a smile. "Do you find it entertaining?"

"Not entertaining," Elysia said, her words coming more easily now. She let her gaze drift briefly to the swirling figures on the dance floor, the glimmer of glass magic weaving through the air. "Beautiful."

Rilian's smile deepened, though it didn't reach his eyes. "And yet, you stay in the shadows. Why?"

The question hit her like a shard of ice.

She hesitated, the hum of the mask growing louder, sharper. Her pulse roared in her ears, and for a moment, she thought the mask might falter, that its cracks might surface beneath the weight of his gaze.

"I'm not..." She paused, choosing her words carefully. "I'm not accustomed to being seen."

The prince studied her for a long moment, his expression unreadable. "Perhaps you should try it."

Elysia's breath hitched. The hum of the mask was deafening now, a vibration that seemed to rattle her very bones. She pressed her hands to her sides, forcing herself to breathe, to hold steady.

Don't falter.

"I might," she said softly, her voice laced with a quiet resolve she hadn't expected. "When the time is right."

Something flickered in Rilian's eyes—curiosity, perhaps—but he didn't press further.

Instead, he stepped closer, his movements slow and deliberate. The crowd seemed to part around him, their attention turning elsewhere, as though the moment between them existed outside of time.

"You wear a mask," he said, his voice quieter now, meant only for her. "But, it doesn't hide you."

Elysia's chest tightened. The mask hummed fiercely, its pull sharp and insistent, and she felt as though the air around her had grown thin.

Rilian tilted his head slightly, his gaze softening but losing none of its intensity. "Who are you?"

The question hung in the air, heavy and fragile.

Elysia's mind raced, her pulse hammering against the pull of the mask. She could feel its strain now, the cracks in its magic trembling at the edges of her control. But, she couldn't falter—not here, not now.

She smiled faintly, tilting her head just enough to let the light catch the edges of the mask. "Someone who doesn't belong."

The prince's expression didn't change, but his gaze lingered, searching hers.

"I disagree," he said softly.

Before she could respond, a loud crash shattered the moment. A glass sculpture near the edge of the ballroom had splintered, sending shards scattering across the floor. Gasps rippled through the crowd as servants hurried to clean the mess, their magic weaving the pieces back together.

The noise jolted Elysia back to herself, her breath coming in short, shallow bursts. She took a step back, the hum of the mask quieting but its weight still heavy against her skin.

Rilian glanced toward the commotion, his brow furrowing faintly, but when he turned back, she was already slipping into the crowd.

Her steps quickened as she moved away from the dais, the voices of the nobles swirling around her like static. Her hands trembled beneath her cloak, and she clutched its edges tightly, her chest aching from the strain of the mask.

But despite the tension, a faint spark lingered in her chest, a quiet exhilaration that refused to fade.

He had seen her.

And he hadn't looked away.

CHAPTER 12

THREADS BEGIN TO UNRAVEL

The murmur of voices swirled around her like the hum of distant bees. Elysia moved carefully through the crowd, her cloak still wrapped loosely around her shoulders, the faint shimmer of her gown catching the light with every step.

The ballroom was alive with energy—laughter, music, and the soft crackle of glass magic weaving through the air. Yet, as Elysia passed, the noise seemed to fade, replaced by whispers that clung to her like a second shadow.

"Have you seen her mask? It's unlike anything I've ever seen."

"Do you think she's from Solmaris?"

"Or another kingdom entirely?"

The voices grew louder as she neared the center of the room, curious and sharp-edged. Elysia kept her head high, her hands steady on the edges of her cloak, though her heart thundered in her chest.

The mask hummed faintly against her skin, its vibration a constant reminder of the magic holding her together.

Stay calm, she told herself. You belong here tonight.

A ripple of light caught her eye, and her gaze flicked toward a group of nobles gathered near the dance floor. A young woman conjured a bloom of glass petals that floated into the air, their edges glowing faintly before dissolving into glittering sparks. The crowd applauded, their voices rising in admiration as the woman bowed gracefully.

The display was breathtaking, but Elysia barely noticed. Her attention was drawn elsewhere—to the edge of the dance floor, where two familiar figures stood.

Vivienne and Alessa.

They were radiant, their gowns glowing like jewels in the light of the chandeliers. Alessa's butterflies hovered above her in delicate arcs, their wings catching the light with every movement. Vivienne's roses twined around her shoulders, their sharp-edged petals shimmering like molten rubies.

Both of them were watching her.

Elysia's breath hitched. She forced herself to look away, her steps quickening as she moved further into the crowd. She could feel their eyes on her, sharp and unrelenting, like blades poised to strike.

"They're saying she's wearing glass." Vivienne's voice carried faintly through the hum of the crowd.

"And glowing," Alessa replied, her tone tinged with envy. "No one glows like that. It's—unnatural."

Vivienne's laughter was low, almost mocking. "Whoever she is, she's trying too hard. The prince won't be fooled for long."

Elysia clenched her fists beneath her cloak, the fabric pulling tight against her fingers. The hum of the mask grew louder, a vibration that seemed to echo their words, pressing against her chest like a warning.

She glanced toward the mirrors lining the walls, catching a brief glimpse of her reflection. The mask was flawless, her face smooth and unrecognizable, but the weight of their gazes made her doubt what she saw.

They don't know it's you, she reminded herself again, fiercely. They can't.

The crowd shifted around her, a swirl of colors and voices that seemed to press closer with every moment. Elysia moved carefully through the gaps, keeping her head high and her steps measured.

"She's hiding something," Vivienne said, her voice sharper now.

Alessa's reply was softer, but no less cutting. "She thinks the mask will protect her. But, magic like that doesn't last."

Elysia's chest tightened. The mask hummed louder still, its pull sharper, more insistent. She could feel the edges of her strength fraying, the strain of holding her composure threatening to unravel her.

Not yet, she thought. Just a little longer.

The whispers around her grew louder, the crowd's curiosity folding over itself in waves.

"Who is she?"

"Her gown looks like glass—do you think she's from the court?"

"I've never seen her before. She must be someone important."

Elysia caught her reflection in the mirrors again, her image flickering faintly as though the light around her had shifted. Her heart skipped a beat, but when she looked closer, the mask was still in place, its magic holding strong.

A faint spark of resolve lit in her chest.

They didn't know. They couldn't see her.

As long as the mask held, she would remain untouchable.

Elysia took another steadying breath and stepped toward the edge of the crowd, her cloak sweeping behind her like a shadow. The hum of the mask steadied, its pull softening as she moved further from her stepsisters' gaze.

But, she knew it wouldn't be long before they found her again.

The music swelled, a waltz that filled the ballroom with light and motion. Elysia stood at the edge of the crowd, her cloak still draped over her shoulders, the mask humming faintly against her skin.

She kept her gaze low, her breathing steady, but every part of her was aware of him.

Prince Rilian stood at the center of the ballroom, his figure unmistakable amid the swirl of nobles. His deep blue coat caught the light of the chandeliers, the silver threads woven into its edges gleaming faintly with each subtle movement. Though surrounded by courtiers, he seemed untouched by the chaos around him, his focus sharp and deliberate.

And then, he moved.

Elysia's breath caught as he turned toward her, his gaze locking onto hers with quiet precision. The mask's hum deepened, its vibration sharp and insistent, as though it sensed the weight of his attention.

The crowd parted easily for him, the nobles stepping aside with murmured bows and curious glances. The waltz continued, its rhythm unbroken, but the focus of the room shifted with him.

Elysia's pulse roared in her ears.

Stay calm. Hold steady.

He stopped just a few feet away, his dark eyes meeting hers with an intensity that made her heart skip a beat.

"Will you dance with me?" His voice was calm, low, but it carried easily over the music, silencing the crowd around them.

Elysia's throat tightened. She could feel every gaze in the room turning toward her, their curiosity pressing against her like a living thing. The mask hummed louder, a sharp vibration that threatened to steal her breath.

"I…" She hesitated, her voice caught in her chest. You can't refuse him.

Slowly, she raised her head, letting the light catch the edges of her mask as she met his gaze. "I would be honored."

His lips curved into a faint smile. He extended his hand, his movements graceful and deliberate, and for a moment, the mask's hum seemed to soften, its pull anchoring her.

Elysia reached out, her gloved fingers brushing against his as he led her toward the center of the ballroom. The whispers rose around them, soft and sharp.

"Who is she?"

"Why would the prince choose her?"

"Look at that mask—it's almost like glass."

Her stepsisters' voices cut through the noise, sharper and closer than the rest.

"Look at her gown," Alessa muttered, her tone dripping with envy. "Whoever she is, she's clearly trying too hard."

Vivienne's voice was quieter, colder. "There's something wrong about her."

The words struck like a knife, but Elysia didn't falter. She let the prince guide her onto the dance floor, her steps measured and steady despite the tension curling in her chest.

The waltz shifted, its rhythm slowing as the crowd stepped back to give them space.

Rilian turned to face her fully, his hand resting lightly against hers, the other at her waist. His touch was warm, steady, and for a moment, she felt as though the rest of the room had melted away.

The music began again, and they moved.

The first steps were tentative, but as the rhythm steadied, so did she. The glass gown flowed around her like liquid light, catching the chandeliers' glow with every movement. The mask hummed faintly, its pull a constant reminder of the magic that bound her, but she pushed the sensation aside, focusing instead on the prince.

"You're very quiet," he said after a moment, his voice low enough that only she could hear.

Elysia met his gaze, her breath catching. "Perhaps I don't have much to say."

His lips curved into a faint smile. "Or perhaps you have too much to hide."

Her heart skipped a beat. The mask's hum deepened, its vibration sharp and insistent, and for a moment, she thought the edges of her vision blurred.

"I think everyone here has something to hide," she said softly, her voice steady despite the pressure in her chest.

"Perhaps," he said, his gaze searching hers. "But, you're not like the rest of them."

The words struck her harder than she expected, their weight sinking deep into her chest. She averted her gaze, focusing on the rhythm of their steps, the way the floor seemed to shimmer beneath their feet.

The music swelled, and Rilian tilted his head slightly, his eyes never leaving her face. "Who are you?" he asked quietly.

Elysia hesitated, the question cutting through her like a blade.

"I'm no one," she said finally, her voice almost a whisper.

His brow furrowed faintly, as though the answer didn't satisfy him. "I don't believe that."

Her pulse roared in her ears, the mask's hum becoming a steady roar. The edges of her control frayed, the pull of the magic growing sharper with each passing moment.

Hold together.

The music swirled around them, the ballroom fading into a haze of light and sound. For a moment, it felt as though the rest of the world had fallen away, leaving only the two of them.

"You remind me of something," Rilian said softly, his

voice breaking the stillness between them. "Something I thought I'd lost."

Elysia's breath hitched.

The final notes of the waltz echoed through the room, their sound lingering in the air like the memory of a dream. Rilian stepped back, his hand lingering on hers for just a moment longer than necessary.

The crowd's murmurs returned, their voices filling the space left by the music. Elysia glanced toward the edge of the room, her stepsisters' faces sharp and intent, their gazes locked on her.

The mask hummed louder, its pull heavy and insistent, and she knew she couldn't stay here much longer.

"I should go," she said softly, pulling her hand free.

Rilian's brow furrowed, but he didn't stop her. "Will I see you again?"

She didn't answer. Instead, she stepped back, her cloak sweeping around her as she disappeared into the crowd.

Her breath came in short, shallow bursts, her chest aching from the strain of the mask. But, her mind clung to his words, their weight echoing in her chest.

"You remind me of something I thought I'd lost."

The edges of the ballroom were quieter, the noise of music and laughter muffled by the heavy drapes and mirrored walls. Elysia slipped into the shadows, her breath coming in short, shallow bursts.

Her chest ached, the mask's hum vibrating through her like a storm building just beneath her skin. She pressed a hand to her heart, her fingers trembling against the fabric of her cloak.

Hold together, she thought desperately. Just hold together a little longer.

She glanced toward the center of the room, where the waltz had ended and the crowd had surged back into motion. Prince Rilian stood beneath the towering glass crest, his dark eyes scanning the crowd, his expression thoughtful.

Her pulse quickened as his gaze brushed past her. He didn't stop, didn't see her hidden in the shadows, but she could still feel the weight of his attention lingering like a phantom touch.

You remind me of something I thought I'd lost.

The words echoed in her mind, sharp and heavy, their meaning twisting in ways she couldn't unravel.

The mask hummed again, sharper this time, and she stumbled, catching herself against the wall. Her reflection flickered faintly in the mirrored glass, the edges of her image blurring for just a moment before settling again.

Panic clawed at her chest.

It's cracking. The magic is cracking.

The voices of the ballroom swirled around her, sharp and disorienting. She moved quickly, her steps unsteady, her chest aching from the strain of the mask.

When she reached the edge of the room, she paused, pressing a hand to her chest as she leaned against the cool glass of a nearby window. Her breath came in ragged gasps, the mask's hum finally softening, though its weight still pressed against her.

Elysia closed her eyes, her fingers brushing against the

edges of the mask. For a moment, she considered tearing it off, letting the magic shatter and the truth spill out into the open.

But, the memory of Rilian's gaze stopped her.

She straightened, pulling her cloak tighter around her shoulders.

She couldn't break now. Not yet.

She turned toward the ballroom, her steps slower but steadier, her gaze fixed on the shimmering chandeliers above.

The night wasn't over.

CHAPTER 13

BENEATH THE GLASS

The music and laughter in the ballroom swirled together into an oppressive din that pressed against Elysia's chest. She lingered near one of the mirrored walls, the shadows of the grand drapes offering her a fragile refuge.

The whispers followed her.

"Who is she?"

"Why won't she tell us her name?"

"That mask—it's almost alive."

Elysia kept her head high, her cloak draped loosely around her shoulders, but her hands trembled beneath its folds. The mask's vibration was sharp and insistent, as though it were warning her that time was slipping away.

Across the room, Vivienne and Alessa stood close together, their voices a faint murmur amid the noise. Vivienne's dark eyes flicked toward Elysia, sharp and unblinking, and Elysia felt the weight of her gaze like a blade pressed against her skin.

"She's watching us again," Vivienne said, her voice low but biting.

Alessa frowned, her golden gown shimmering faintly in the light of the chandeliers. "You're imagining things. She's probably just another desperate court girl hoping for the prince's attention."

"Desperate?" Vivienne's lips curled into a smile that held no warmth. "Desperation doesn't hum with magic. Look at her, Alessa. Look closely. That mask, that gown... it's unnatural."

Alessa hesitated, her gaze flicking toward Elysia before darting away again. "She's certainly overdressed," she muttered.

Vivienne's smile sharpened. "Overdressed—and hiding something."

Lady Seraphine joined them then, her emerald gown trailing like a shadow behind her. She followed Vivienne's gaze, her sharp features tightening as her eyes settled on Elysia.

"What nonsense are you whispering about now?" she asked, though her tone carried more curiosity than dismissal.

"There's something wrong about her," Vivienne said, her voice soft but deliberate. "Don't you feel it?"

Lady Seraphine studied Elysia for a long moment, her expression unreadable. "Whoever she is, she's clearly of some importance," she said finally. "The prince doesn't waste his time on just anyone."

"That's what I mean," Vivienne pressed. "Why would he notice her unless there's something... off about her?"

"Or something familiar," Alessa added quietly.

Elysia's pulse quickened. She turned her head, pretending to admire the mirrors as her chest tightened beneath the weight of their words.

They don't know it's you. They can't.

But, the mask's vibration rattled through her bones, and she could feel the edges of her composure slipping.

Vivienne's voice rose slightly, her tone sharpening. "Why don't we just ask her?"

Elysia's breath hitched. She turned slightly, catching Vivienne's reflection in the mirror—a sleek, elegant figure with eyes like daggers. Vivienne stepped away from her family, her movements slow and deliberate, her gaze locked on Elysia.

The crowd around them began to quiet, their murmurs fading into a curious hush as they followed Vivienne's line of sight.

"Who are you?" Vivienne's voice carried easily over the music, low but unmistakably pointed.

Elysia's fingers curled into fists beneath her cloak. She met Vivienne's gaze head-on, her chin lifting slightly as she forced herself to speak.

"I don't believe I've had the pleasure of an introduction," she said, her voice steady despite the hammering of her heart.

Vivienne's smile returned, cold and razor-sharp. "You haven't."

The nobles around them stilled, their gazes darting between the two women. Even Alessa looked uneasy now, her brow furrowing as she watched the exchange.

Lady Seraphine said nothing, but her presence loomed just behind Vivienne, her sharp eyes taking in every detail.

The mask hummed louder, its vibration skittering across Elysia's skin like the edge of a storm. She straightened her shoulders, her fingers tightening on the edges of her cloak.

"I don't see why my name matters," she said quietly. "The ball is for everyone, isn't it?"

Vivienne tilted her head, her smile faltering just enough to show a flash of irritation. "For everyone, perhaps," she said. "But, the prince doesn't dance with just anyone."

The murmurs returned, softer now, but sharper.

"Is she a foreign noble?"

"Why won't she just say who she is?"

"Do you think she's enchanted?"

Elysia's chest tightened. The mask's hum deepened, as though it were warning her that she couldn't withstand this much longer.

Vivienne took another step closer, her voice dropping to a near whisper. "You feel familiar," she said, her eyes narrowing. "Why is that?"

Elysia forced a calm smile, though her hands trembled beneath her cloak. "Perhaps you've seen me in a dream," she said lightly.

Vivienne's smile faded entirely, her gaze hardening. "I don't dream of shadows."

The words cut deep, but Elysia didn't falter. She turned slightly, the motion catching the light of the chandeliers and sending a shimmer across her gown.

"Perhaps you should," she said softly.

The crowd murmured again, their curiosity growing,

but before Vivienne could respond, a flicker of movement caught Elysia's eye.

Prince Rilian.

He was crossing the ballroom, his expression calm but purposeful, his gaze sweeping past the crowd to rest directly on her.

Elysia's breath caught. The mask hummed louder, its pull sharp and insistent, but she stood her ground as the prince approached.

Vivienne turned as well, her irritation deepening into something closer to anger. But when Rilian reached them, she stepped back with a stiff curtsy.

The prince ignored her. His dark eyes settled on Elysia, their quiet intensity cutting through the noise like a blade.

The weight of the ballroom pressed down like a held breath. Elysia stood frozen, her hands hidden within the folds of her cloak, as Prince Rilian's voice cut through the growing murmurs.

"Will you join me?"

His words were simple, steady, but they carried a weight that silenced the crowd. The nobles' whispers died away, their gazes shifting from Vivienne to the prince, their curiosity sharpening like glass.

Elysia hesitated, her pulse roaring in her ears. She could feel Vivienne's eyes burning into her, her suspicion coiled like a snake ready to strike. The mask hummed faintly against her skin, its pull sharp but not unbearable—yet.

"I would be honored," Elysia said softly, forcing her voice to remain calm.

Rilian extended his hand, his dark eyes never leaving hers. For a moment, she hesitated, the air between them taut with unspoken tension. Then, she reached out, placing her trembling fingers lightly in his.

His hand was warm, steady, grounding.

The crowd parted before them as Rilian led her toward the grand staircase at the edge of the ballroom. The murmurs returned, soft and sharp, their curiosity a wave that rippled through the room.

"Who is she?"

"The prince hasn't done that for anyone before."

"Do you think she's enchanted?"

Vivienne's voice cut through the whispers, low but biting. "A mystery isn't the same as a miracle."

Elysia didn't look back, but the venom in Vivienne's words sank into her chest like a shard of ice. The mask's vibration was sharp against her temples, but she focused on Rilian's steady presence, on the quiet authority in his stride.

At the base of the staircase, he stopped and turned to face her. The nobles around them stilled, their gazes fixed on the pair as though the very air between them carried secrets waiting to be revealed.

"You're drawing attention," Rilian said quietly, his voice low enough that only she could hear.

Elysia's breath hitched. The mask trembled faintly against her skin, its magic pressing against the edges of her composure.

"So are you," she replied softly.

The faintest smile tugged at his lips, though his gaze remained serious. He tilted his head slightly, his eyes searching hers with a quiet intensity that made her chest tighten.

"You're not like them," he said. "And they know it."

Elysia's pulse quickened. The mask's hum grew sharper, as though it were reacting to the weight of his words.

"Perhaps I'm exactly like them," she said, her voice steadier than she expected.

Rilian studied her for a long moment, his brow furrowing faintly as though considering her response. Then, he extended his hand again, his movements slow and deliberate, his gaze never leaving hers.

"Come with me," he said, his voice calm but resolute. "There's a quieter place where we can speak."

The crowd's murmurs surged again, their voices a tide of curiosity and speculation. Elysia hesitated, the weight of their gazes pressing against her like a physical force.

"I..." Her voice faltered. The mask's hum was deafening now, its pull dragging at her strength, but she forced herself to nod. "Of course."

Rilian's hand lingered just long enough to steady her before he turned, leading her up the grand staircase. The crowd below watched with rapt attention, their whispers growing louder with every step.

Vivienne's voice cut through the noise once more, sharp and accusing. "She's hiding something!"

The words rang out like a bell, freezing Elysia in place.

Her breath hitched, the mask's hum faltering for just a moment, and she felt the faintest flicker of magic ripple across her reflection in the mirrors lining the staircase.

Rilian stopped, his head turning slightly as he cast a glance over his shoulder. His expression didn't change, but his presence seemed to shift, his calm exterior hardening into something sharper, more commanding.

"The only thing she's hiding," he said, his voice carrying easily across the room, "is her patience for unwarranted accusations."

Gasps and laughter swept through the crowd, and Vivienne's face darkened, her lips pressing into a thin line.

Elysia's heart pounded in her chest, the mask trembling faintly against her skin. But, the prince didn't look at her again. He simply extended his hand, his steady presence anchoring her once more.

"Shall we?" he asked softly.

Elysia nodded, her movements slow and deliberate as she placed her hand in his. Together, they ascended the staircase, leaving the murmurs and tension of the ballroom behind.

The mask's hum softened, but its weight lingered, pressing against her chest like an unspoken warning.

This isn't over.

The alcove was quiet, tucked away from the main ballroom and shielded by a pair of heavy velvet curtains. A faint glow from a glass chandelier above bathed the space in soft light, the edges of the walls lined with mirrors that seemed to stretch the room into infinity.

Elysia stood near the center, her hands clasped tightly beneath the folds of her cloak. The hum of the mask was quieter here, but its weight lingered, pressing against her temples and chest with a steady insistence.

Prince Rilian lingered near the entrance, his gaze steady as he studied her. The weight of his attention was palpable, a force that seemed to crackle through the air between them.

"You're nervous," he said finally, his voice soft but certain.

Elysia hesitated, her pulse quickening. "Why would I be?" she asked, though her voice sounded smaller than she intended.

He stepped closer, his movements slow and deliberate, his dark eyes narrowing faintly. "Perhaps because you feel as though the world is waiting for you to falter."

Her breath caught. The mask hummed louder, a sharp vibration that sent a shiver down her spine. She looked away, her gaze catching on her reflection in one of the mirrors. For a moment, the edges of her image flickered, the light distorting faintly before settling again.

"I didn't ask to be noticed," she said softly.

Rilian's lips curved into the faintest hint of a smile. "No, I suppose you didn't."

He stopped just a few feet away, his hands clasped loosely behind his back. There was no hostility in his gaze, no judgment—but there was something sharper beneath it, something searching.

"You remind me of something," he said after a moment, his voice quieter now. "Or someone. But I can't quite place it."

Elysia's chest tightened. The mask's pull was sharper now, more insistent. Her breath came in shallow bursts.

"I'm no one," she said finally, her voice trembling slightly.

Rilian's brow furrowed, his expression thoughtful. "No one doesn't catch the attention of an entire room. No one doesn't move through the court like a shadow and leave whispers in their wake."

Her hands tightened further, her nails digging into her palms. She could feel the edges of her strength slipping, the mask's magic pressing against her like a storm waiting to break.

"You don't know anything about me," she said, her voice sharper now, though the tremor in it betrayed her vulnerability.

"Perhaps not," he said, his tone steady but piercing. "But, I'd like to."

The words hung in the air between them, heavy and fragile.

Elysia turned away, her cloak sweeping against the floor as she moved toward the far edge of the alcove. She placed a hand against the cool surface of a mirror, her reflection staring back at her with eyes that seemed too bright, too sharp.

The mask hummed again, its vibration rattling through her bones, and for a moment, she thought she felt it tremble.

"You're afraid," Rilian said quietly, his voice cutting through the silence.

Elysia's breath hitched. She didn't turn to face him.

"I'm not afraid," she said, though the words felt hollow.

"Yes, you are," he said, his footsteps soft as he moved closer. "You're afraid of being seen. Of being known. Why?"

Her chest ached, the mask's pull trying to contain something that refused to be held.

"Because..." She faltered, her voice breaking. She closed her eyes, her fingers tightening against the edge of the mirror. "Because I don't belong here."

The confession slipped out before she could stop it, the words trembling in the air like shards of glass.

Rilian's footsteps stopped, his presence stilling behind her.

"I don't believe that," he said softly.

Elysia opened her eyes, her gaze locking with her reflection. The mask's edges shimmered faintly, the light around it flickering like a candle on the verge of going out.

"You don't understand," she said, her voice barely above a whisper.

"Then help me understand."

The words struck her like a blow, sharp and unyielding. She turned to face him, her breath coming in shallow bursts, her chest tight with the weight of the mask's magic.

For a long moment, neither of them spoke. The air between them was heavy, charged with something unspoken but undeniable.

"I can't," she said finally, her voice trembling. "I can't be what you think I am."

Rilian's expression softened, his gaze steady and unwavering. "What do you think I see?"

Her chest tightened further, the hum of the mask

roaring now, its vibration pressing against her temples like a drumbeat.

You see me, she thought desperately. And, I can't let you.

The mirrors around them shimmered faintly, the light shifting as though the room itself were holding its breath.

Elysia took a step back, her hands trembling as she clutched the edges of her cloak. "I need to go," she said, her voice breaking.

Rilian didn't move, his gaze still fixed on her. "Will I see you again?"

She hesitated, the mask's hum deafening in her ears. Her breath came in ragged gasps, the weight of the moment threatening to pull her under.

"I don't know," she whispered.

Without waiting for a response, she turned and slipped through the curtains, her steps unsteady as she disappeared into the shadows of the palace halls.

The hum of the mask softened, but its weight lingered, pressing against her chest like a wound she couldn't heal.

He saw too much.

CHAPTER 14
CRACKS IN THE GLASS

T he hallways of the palace were quieter, the din of the ballroom fading to a faint hum as Elysia slipped through the velvet curtains and into the shadows beyond. The faint glow of the chandeliers cast her reflection in the polished floors, her glass gown shimmering faintly beneath her cloak.

The mask hummed softly, the sound steady but insistent, like the ticking of a clock she couldn't escape.

Her breath came in shallow bursts as she pressed a hand to her chest, trying to steady the frantic rhythm of her heart. She needed a moment to think, to breathe, to hold herself together before the mask's fragile magic cracked beneath the weight of her fear.

The ballroom was brighter now, the chandeliers casting fractured rainbows across the mirrored walls as the music swelled into a lively reel. Elysia stood just inside the entrance, her breath coming in shallow bursts as she adjusted her cloak.

The mask hummed faintly against her skin, a sharp and steady vibration that seemed to echo her heartbeat. She could feel the tension crackling in the air around her, the weight of whispers and glances pressing against her like a storm on the verge of breaking.

She had barely stepped into the crowd when a sharp voice cut through the din.

"There she is!"

Elysia froze.

Vivienne's voice carried easily over the music, low but commanding, her words drawing the attention of the nearest nobles.

Elysia turned slowly, her pulse roaring in her ears as Vivienne approached, her crimson gown flowing like molten glass. Her dark eyes gleamed with triumph, her smile cold and razor-sharp.

The crowd stilled, their murmurs quieting as they turned to watch. Alessa followed behind Vivienne, her expression uncertain but drawn with reluctant determination.

"You're very difficult to keep track of," Vivienne said, her voice smooth but laced with venom. "Why do you keep running off, I wonder?"

Elysia's chest tightened. The mask's hum grew louder, the vibration pressing against her temples like a blade.

"I don't know what you're talking about," she said, her voice calm despite the tension coiling in her chest.

Vivienne's smile widened, but there was no warmth in it. "Don't you?" She stepped closer, her movements slow and deliberate, her gaze sweeping over Elysia's cloak and mask. "You've been hiding all night, haven't you? Skulking in the shadows, avoiding questions. It makes one wonder what you're afraid of."

The crowd stirred, their whispers growing louder.

"Is she enchanted?"

"Why won't she show her face?"

"She can't be from Solmaris, can she?"

Elysia straightened her shoulders, forcing herself to meet Vivienne's gaze. "I'm not hiding anything," she said, though her voice trembled faintly at the edges.

Vivienne tilted her head, her smile fading into something sharper. "No?" She gestured toward Elysia's cloak, her dark eyes narrowing. "Why don't you show us what's beneath the mask?"

The words struck like a thunderclap, rippling through the crowd. Gasps and murmurs rose around them, the nobles pressing closer, their curiosity sharpening into something more dangerous.

Elysia's hands tightened on the edges of her cloak, her pulse roaring in her ears. The mask hummed louder, its pull heavier now, as though it were struggling to hold her together.

"I don't owe you anything," she said quietly, her voice trembling but resolute.

Vivienne laughed softly, the sound like broken glass. "Oh, but you do. You owe the truth." She stepped closer, her voice dropping to a near whisper. "You're not one of us. You don't belong here, do you?"

Elysia felt her composure slipping, the mask's hum growing erratic as the weight of their suspicion pressed down on her. She took a slow step back, her cloak brushing against the marble floor.

Vivienne's eyes narrowed further, her smile returning as though she sensed the crack in Elysia's armor. "What's wrong?" she asked, her voice dripping with mock concern. "Afraid of being seen?"

The words struck harder than they should have. Elysia's reflection in the nearby window wavered faintly, the edges of the mask's magic flickering like a candle in the wind.

Her pulse roared in her ears, her breath coming faster now. The walls felt as though they were closing in, the weight of the mask's magic pressing against her chest, her very soul.

"You're not going anywhere," Vivienne said, her voice sharp and commanding. "Not until we know the truth."

Elysia's gaze darted past them, toward the faint glow of the ballroom beyond. She could hear the swell of music, the rise and fall of laughter, the low hum of glass magic weaving through the air.

She couldn't go back—not like this. But, she couldn't stay here either, trapped beneath Vivienne's piercing gaze.

The mask trembled again, its hum skittering through her like shards of ice.

Elysia's chest tightened further, her vision blurring faintly as the mask's magic strained against her control.

Not yet, she thought desperately. Not here.

The murmurs grew louder, the crowd pressing closer, their gazes burning against Elysia's skin. She felt the edges of her strength slipping, the mask's magic trembling like a thread stretched too thin.

"Enough."

The single word cut through the noise like a blade.

The crowd stilled, their whispers fading into silence as Prince Rilian stepped forward, his dark eyes fixed on Vivienne.

His presence was commanding, his deep blue coat gleaming faintly in the light of the chandeliers. He moved with quiet authority, his gaze steady and unyielding as he positioned himself between Elysia and her stepsisters.

"That's quite enough," he said again, his voice calm but firm.

Vivienne faltered, her smile flickering as she took a small step back. "Your Highness," she said, her tone carefully measured. "I was only trying to—"

"To what?" Rilian interrupted, his voice low but cutting. "Embarrass her? Shame her? For what crime, exactly?"

Vivienne's expression darkened, her lips pressing into a thin line. "She won't even tell us her name," she said, her voice laced with venom. "Doesn't that seem suspicious to you?"

Rilian's gaze didn't waver. "What seems suspicious to me," he said, his tone cold, "is your determination to humiliate her in front of the entire court."

Murmurs swept through the crowd, their gazes darting between Vivienne and the prince.

Elysia's breath came in shallow bursts, her chest tight with the weight of the mask's magic. The hum had grown deafening now, the vibration pressing against her temples, her chest, her very soul.

Rilian turned slightly, his gaze softening as he looked

at her. "You don't have to answer to them," he said quietly, his voice steady and reassuring.

The words sent a flicker of warmth through her chest, but it was short-lived. She felt the faintest crack shudder through its magic.

Her breath hitched, her vision blurring faintly as the strain threatened to overwhelm her.

Vivienne took a step forward, her voice sharp and unrelenting. "What is she hiding, then?" she demanded. "If she has nothing to fear, why won't she show us who she is?"

Rilian's gaze darkened, his calm exterior hardening into something closer to fury. "You will not speak another word," he said, his tone cold as ice.

Vivienne's mouth opened, then closed, her expression flickering with frustration and barely concealed anger.

The crowd held its collective breath, their eyes fixed on the prince and the mysterious masked girl who stood trembling at his side.

Elysia's chest tightened further, the mask's magic trembling on the edge of collapse. She felt the cracks spreading, the strain pulling her closer to the breaking point.

But for now, she stood tall, the prince's steady presence anchoring her as the storm raged around them.

The ballroom seemed to hold its breath.

Elysia stood at the center of it all, her chest tight, her hands trembling beneath the folds of her cloak. The mask hummed louder now, a sharp vibration that resonated through her very bones. She could feel the cracks spreading, the fragile threads of magic pulling apart with every passing moment.

Prince Rilian stood beside her, his presence steady and unyielding, a barrier against the storm of whispers and accusations swirling around them. But even his calm strength couldn't stop the inevitable.

Vivienne's voice broke the silence, sharp and cutting.

"Why are you protecting her?" she demanded, her dark eyes blazing with anger. "What has she done to deserve it? Look at her!" She gestured toward Elysia with a sweep of her hand, her tone rising with every word. "She hides behind that mask, that cloak, refusing to show us who she is. What is she afraid of?"

The crowd murmured in agreement, their voices a tide of curiosity and doubt that pressed against Elysia like a weight she could no longer bear.

The mask's hum deepened, its vibration turning into a low, ominous crackle.

Rilian turned toward her, his gaze steady but searching. "You don't have to do this alone," he said softly, his voice cutting through the noise like a blade.

Elysia's breath hitched. She wanted to believe him, wanted to lean into the quiet strength of his words. But, the mask's magic was failing, the cracks spreading faster now, the pull of the truth too strong to resist.

She took a step back, her hands clutching at the edges of her cloak as though it could shield her from what was coming.

"I..." Her voice trembled, breaking under the weight of the moment. "I can't—"

The mask cracked.

A sharp, splintering sound echoed through the ballroom, loud and clear as shattering glass. The crowd gasped, their murmurs rising into a crescendo of shock and awe as the magic unraveled in a burst of light.

Elysia's knees buckled, the weight of the magic crashing down on her like a tidal wave. She fell to the ground, her cloak sweeping around her as shards of the mask's light spiraled through the air.

Pain bloomed along her cheek as the edges of the mask fractured and splintered. Tiny, sharp cuts bit into her skin, warm streaks of blood mingling with the faint glow of magic still clinging to the shards. She pressed a trembling hand to her face, the sting of the injuries drowned out by the overwhelming pull of the magic's collapse.

When the light faded, the room fell into stunned silence.

Elysia knelt in the center of the ballroom, her face exposed, her gown glowing faintly with the remnants of the mask's magic. Her breath came in shallow bursts, her chest aching with the strain of the collapse.

The crowd stared, their faces a mixture of awe, confusion, and fear.

Vivienne was the first to speak, her voice cold and sharp. "It's you," she hissed, her expression twisting with shock and fury. "It's you."

Alessa's hand flew to her mouth, her golden butterflies trembling faintly in the air around her. "Elysia?" she whispered, her voice barely audible.

Elysia didn't move. She couldn't. The weight of their

gazes pressed against her, the raw edges of the mask's magic lingering like a wound she couldn't hide.

Rilian stepped forward, his movements slow and deliberate. His dark eyes softened as he knelt before her, his presence a calm anchor in the chaos.

"Is this why you were afraid?" he asked quietly, his voice steady but laced with something deeper—something like understanding.

Elysia's breath hitched. She looked up at him, her eyes wide and filled with unshed tears. "I didn't want you to see me like this," she whispered, her voice breaking.

He reached out, his hand hovering just above hers. "Why?"

"Because I'm not…" She faltered, her throat tightening. "I'm not what you think I am. I'm not… enough."

Rilian's gaze didn't waver. He lowered his hand, his fingers brushing against hers with a touch so gentle it felt like a promise.

"You're more than enough," he said softly.

The words sent a shiver through her, the warmth of his presence wrapping around her like a shield against the cold.

But, the moment was short-lived.

Lady Seraphine stepped forward, her emerald gown gleaming in the fractured light. Her sharp voice rang out like a bell, cutting through the quiet.

"Explain yourself," she demanded, her eyes narrowing on Elysia. "What is this magic? Who are you, truly?"

CHAPTER 15

BREAKING THE GLASS CAGE

The chamber was cold and quiet, its mirrored walls casting distorted reflections of the nobles who had gathered within. The air was thick with tension, the weight of unspoken questions pressing down on Elysia like a shroud.

She stood at the center of the room, her hands trembling at her sides. Her glass gown shimmered faintly in the low light, but the glow that had once felt like a shield now felt more like a spotlight, exposing every crack in her armor.

Elysia swallowed hard, her gaze flicking toward Prince Rilian, who stood beside her, his presence calm but watchful. His dark eyes met hers with quiet encouragement, and she drew strength from the steadiness of his gaze.

At the far end of the chamber, Vivienne and Alessa lingered near Lady Seraphine, their expressions a mix of anger and triumph. The other nobles whispered among themselves, their curiosity sharpened into suspicion as they waited for Elysia to speak.

"I..." Elysia's voice faltered, her breath hitching as she tried to find the words. Her nails bit into her palms. "I owe you the truth."

The murmurs quieted, the room growing still as every gaze turned toward her.

"My name is Elysia," she began, her voice trembling but growing stronger with each word. "And I am the last of a family cursed by its own ambition."

The nobles gasped, their whispers rising again.

Rilian stepped forward, raising a hand to silence the crowd. His voice was calm but commanding. "Let her finish."

Elysia nodded, her chest tightening as she continued. "Years ago, my family struck a bargain with a powerful glass mage—a pact sealed with forbidden magic. They wanted power, status, everything this kingdom values above all else. They were willing to pay any price for it."

Her voice broke, but she forced herself to go on. "But, when the time came to honor their end of the bargain, they refused. My mother broke her promise, and the mage... he cursed us for her betrayal."

She glanced toward one of the mirrors lining the walls, her own reflection staring back at her with haunted eyes. The glass shimmered faintly, as though the magic within it could feel her words.

"The curse stripped us of our magic, our status, our place in this kingdom," she said. "It made us invisible, powerless. And, it ensured that we could never rise again."

Lady Seraphine stepped forward, her emerald gown trailing behind her like a shadow. Her sharp eyes narrowed on Elysia. "And the mage? What became of him?"

Elysia hesitated, her pulse quickening. "He..." Her voice caught, her chest tightening with the weight of the truth. "He was bound to the mirrors, imprisoned by his own magic. His power became his cage."

Shock swept through the room, the nobles' whispers turning into a storm of questions.

"And you?" Vivienne's voice cut through the noise, sharp and accusing. "What have you done to change any of this? You've been hiding, haven't you? Hiding while the rest of us pay the price for your family's mistakes."

Elysia flinched, her hands tightening into fists. "I didn't choose this," she said, her voice trembling with anger and pain. "I didn't choose to be cursed, to live as a shadow. But, I've spent my life trying to find a way to break it."

"And have you?" Lady Seraphine demanded, her voice cold. "Do you have a solution to this curse, or are we merely here to listen to your excuses?"

Elysia's breath hitched. She glanced toward Rilian, his steady presence grounding her.

"I do," she said finally, her voice quiet but firm. "But, breaking the curse won't just free my family. It will free him."

The room fell into stunned silence.

Vivienne's eyes narrowed, her lips curling into a sneer. "Why should we care about freeing a mage who cursed you in the first place?"

"Because the curse doesn't end with me," Elysia said, her voice rising. "It has seeped into the very fabric of this kingdom. The magic you use, the power you value—it's all tied to him, to his imprisonment. Breaking the curse isn't just about me. It's about all of us."

The crowd erupted into chaos, their voices clashing in a storm of fear, anger, and confusion.

Lady Seraphine raised her hands, her voice cutting through the noise like a blade. "Enough!" She turned to Elysia, her expression unreadable. "If what you say is true, then the stakes are higher than any of us imagined. But, I wonder..." Her gaze sharpened. "Are you willing to pay the price to end this? Or will you follow in your family's footsteps and run from it?"

Elysia's chest tightened, her breath trembling as she met Lady Seraphine's piercing gaze.

"I'm not running," she said, her voice steady despite the storm inside her. "I'll do whatever it takes to break the curse, even if it means sacrificing everything I have left."

The room fell silent again, the weight of her words settling over the gathered nobles.

Rilian stepped forward, his voice calm but resolute. "Then, we'll face it together," he said, his gaze steady as it met hers. "You don't have to do this alone."

Elysia's heart swelled, a flicker of warmth breaking through the tension. She nodded, her resolve hardening.

The time for hiding was over.

The hall of mirrors was alive with light.

The glass stretched endlessly in all directions, reflecting and refracting the faint glow of the chandeliers into a kaleidoscope of brilliance. Each step Elysia took sent ripples through the air, her glass gown shimmering faintly in the fractured light.

Beside her, Rilian moved with quiet purpose, his presence a steadying force against the storm swirling within her. Ahead of them, at the heart of the chamber, the largest mirror stood like a portal, its surface dark and vibrating with latent power.

And there, bound within the glass, was Caius.

His reflection flickered faintly, his figure half-formed as though caught between two worlds. His eyes, sharp and glittering, followed their every move, his presence radiating a cold, ancient power that made the air feel heavy.

"You've come," Caius said, his voice low and smooth, echoing through the chamber. "I wondered how long you would linger in the shadows before stepping into the light."

Elysia stopped a few paces from the mirror, her breath catching as her reflection shimmered beside his. "I didn't come to listen to your taunts," she said, her voice steady despite the tremor in her chest.

Caius tilted his head, a faint smile curling his lips. "No, I suppose you didn't. You came to bargain. To beg. To break what you cannot possibly understand."

Rilian stepped forward, his voice calm but firm. "She came to end this. Whatever power you have over her—over this kingdom—ends tonight."

Caius's laughter was low and cold, rippling through the mirrored chamber like shards of ice. "Such bold words for someone who doesn't yet know the cost."

The light in the mirrors flickered as Caius turned his attention back to Elysia.

"You think breaking the curse will free you," he said softly. "But, it won't. Freedom comes at a price, and this price is higher than you can imagine."

Elysia's hands tightened into fists at her sides. "I don't care about the price," she said. "I'll pay it, whatever it is."

Caius's smile widened, his reflection shimmering faintly as he gestured toward the mirrors around them. "Do you see this prison?" he asked, his voice laced with mockery. "Every shard of glass in this kingdom is a piece of me. Every glimmer of magic is bound to my will. To shatter the curse is to shatter me. But, it will also shatter you."

Her breath hitched. "What do you mean?"

"You're bound to this magic as much as I am," Caius said, his voice low and sharp. "The glass you wield, the power you've claimed—it's a part of you now. To destroy the curse is to destroy your magic. Your bond. Your very essence."

The words struck like a blow, the weight of them settling heavily on her chest.

Rilian stepped closer, his voice quiet but steady. "You don't have to listen to him," he said. "This curse doesn't define you. You're more than the magic it gave you."

Elysia turned toward him, her breath trembling. "What if he's right? What if I lose everything? What if..." She hesitated, her voice breaking. "What if I lose you?"

Rilian's gaze softened, his dark eyes steady as he reached for her hand. "You won't lose me," he said. "Not now, not ever."

The warmth of his touch steadied her, and she drew a shaky breath, her resolve hardening. She turned back to Caius, her gaze fierce.

"What happens to you if the curse is broken?" she asked.

Caius's smile faltered. "I am freed," he said, his voice quieter now. "But, freedom is not the mercy you think it is. Without the curse, I am nothing. A hollow shell of the power I once wielded."

"And the kingdom?" she pressed. "What happens to it?"

Caius's expression darkened. "The glass-bound magic will shatter. The nobles will lose their toys. The balance of power will shift." His voice turned cold again. "But, it is your choice to make. Will you cling to the illusion of power? Or will you sacrifice it all for a chance at something real?"

The mirrors around them shimmered faintly, their light flickering like a heartbeat. The weight of the moment pressed down on her.

Elysia stepped forward, her reflection merging with Caius's in the surface of the mirror. She placed her hand against the cold glass, her breath trembling.

"I won't let this curse define me," she said softly. "And, I won't let it control this kingdom any longer."

The light in the mirror flared, the ripples turning into sharp cracks that splintered across the glass.

Caius's voice rose, sharp and furious. "You don't know what you're doing!"

"I know enough," Elysia said.

She clenched her hand into a fist, and with a single, decisive motion, she struck the mirror.

The glass shattered in a burst of light and sound, the shards spiraling outward like a storm of stars. The chamber trembled, the mirrors cracking and collapsing around them as the magic unraveled.

Elysia fell to her knees, the weight of the curse crashing down on her in a wave of pain and light. Her chest burned, her breath hitching as the remnants of the glass magic faded from her body.

When the light dimmed, the chamber was silent.

Caius's reflection was gone, the mirrors reduced to fragments that glittered faintly on the floor. The weight of the magic had lifted, leaving the air lighter, freer.

Elysia looked up, her breath trembling, her body aching with the loss of the magic that had once been a part of her.

Rilian knelt beside her, his hands steady as he cupped her face. "You did it," he said softly, his voice filled with quiet awe.

She nodded, tears streaming down her face. "It's over," she whispered. "It's finally over."

The palace gardens were still, the faint light of dawn spilling over the horizon and casting the world in soft hues of gold and lavender. The air was cool, carrying the scent of earth and flowers, and for the first time in years, Elysia felt as though she could breathe.

She stood at the edge of the garden's reflecting pool,

the water still and clear, showing no trace of the fractured glass magic that had haunted her for so long. The remnants of her gown shimmered faintly in the morning light, its once-glowing threads dulled but no less beautiful.

Her fingers brushed the surface of the water, sending ripples across her reflection. It was just her now—no mask, no magic, no illusions.

The sound of footsteps drew her attention, and she turned to see Rilian approaching. His coat was undone, his hair slightly tousled, but his dark eyes were steady, soft with relief and something deeper.

"I wondered where you'd gone," he said, his voice quiet in the stillness.

"I needed a moment," she replied, her voice calm but carrying the weight of the night's events. "To think. To feel... everything."

Rilian nodded, stepping closer. He didn't speak right away, simply standing beside her and letting the quiet settle between them.

The first rays of sunlight broke over the trees, painting the garden in warm light. Elysia watched as the world came alive around her, the colors brighter, the air lighter, as though the weight of the curse had lifted not just from her, but from everything.

"It's strange," she said finally, her voice soft. "I thought I'd feel... empty, without the magic. But, I don't."

Rilian tilted his head, his gaze steady. "Why do you think that is?"

She smiled faintly, her fingers trailing through the water again. "Because it was never really mine," she said. "It was something stolen, something forced. And now that it's gone..." She hesitated, her voice trembling with emotion. "Now that it's gone, I finally feel like myself."

Rilian's hand brushed against hers, his touch warm and grounding. "Then, I think you've gained more than you've lost," he said.

Her chest tightened, a quiet ache spreading through her as she looked at him. "I was afraid," she admitted, her voice barely above a whisper. "Afraid that without the magic, without the mask, you'd see me and... turn away."

He frowned, his hand tightening around hers. "Why would you think that?"

"Because I'm not extraordinary," she said, her voice trembling. "I'm not powerful, or beautiful, or... anything the court would expect."

Rilian's brow furrowed, his gaze piercing. "You think I care about what they expect?" he asked, his voice soft but firm. "Elysia, everything I've seen of you—your strength, your kindness, your resolve—is more extraordinary than any magic could ever be."

Her breath hitched, tears welling in her eyes. She tried to speak, but the words caught in her throat, her emotions too raw to shape into sound.

Rilian's hand moved to cup her cheek, his thumb brushing away a stray tear. "You don't need magic to be enough," he said. "You never did."

A quiet sob escaped her, and she leaned into his touch, the warmth of his hand grounding her, anchoring her in the moment.

"I don't know what comes next," she said softly.

"Neither do I," he admitted, a faint smile tugging at his lips. "But whatever it is, I'd like to face it with you."

The words settled over her like a balm, easing the ache in her chest. She nodded, her tears falling freely now, though they were tears of relief, of hope.

The garden seemed to glow brighter as the sun rose higher, its light casting away the last remnants of the night.

For the first time in years, Elysia felt free.

THE END

Did you enjoy Elysia and Rilian's story?
Please rate or review it on Goodreads, Bookbub, or your favourite retailers

Read *A Curse of Silver and Scars*, the next book in the *Legends Reborn* series.

For updates, sales, and promotions, join my newsletter at mhlebeaultauthor.substack.com

About the Author

Positive, uplifting books and stories.

Marie-Hélène Lebeault is the author of *The Evers Series, Clarity Castle, What Happens Next? Readers Decide Which Story Becomes a Book, the Blood Magick Trilogy, Holiday Shifters, Ghost Stories, Defenders of the Realm, Utopia, Chronicles of the Starborne Cadets*, as well as a series of picture books called Fairy Grandmother. She lives in Canada with her grown children.

www.mhlebeault.com

Follow on Social Media, she'd love to hear from you!

facebook.com/mhlebeaultauthor

x.com/mhlebeault

instagram.com/mhlebeault

amazon.com/author/mhlebeault

bookbub.com/authors/marie-helene-lebeault

goodreads.com/mhlebeault

linkedin.com/in/mhlebeault

tiktok.com/@mhlebeaultauthor

ALSO BY THE AUTHOR

A Summer of Courage

The Quest for the Kraken's Ink

A Summer of Destiny

The Quest for the Cursed Mirrors

A Summer of Unity

Defenders of the Realm - Special Edition Hardcover Set

The Battle of the Blossoming Flame (FREE!)

The Evers Series

The Ancestors' Key

The Academy

The Time Walker

The World Jumper

5th Anniversary Edition Omnibus

The Traveler's Handbook

The Lost Key

Blood Magick Trilogy

The Blood Mage

Blood Magick

Blood Legacy

Extended Edition Omnibus

Standalones

Clarity Castle

What Happens Next?

Ghost Stories

Holiday Shifters

Echoes of Tomorrow

Utopia

Picture Books

Fairy Grandmother: Millie Goes to Antarctica

Fairy Grandmother: Millie Goes to the North Pole

Fairy Grandmother: Millie Goes to China

Fairy Grandmother: Millie Goes to Africa

(Also available in French, Spanish, German, and Italian)

www.ingramcontent.com/pod-product-compliance
Lightning Source LLC
Chambersburg PA
CBHW032004240626
47153CB00003B/1120